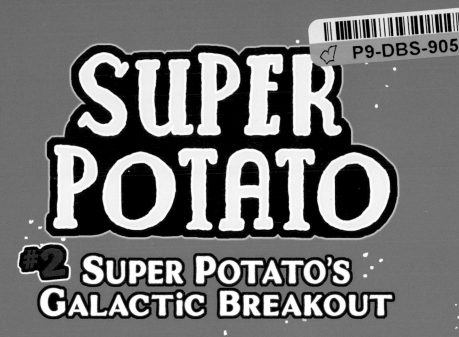

SUPER POTATO

#2 SUPER POTATO'S GALACTIC BREAKOUT

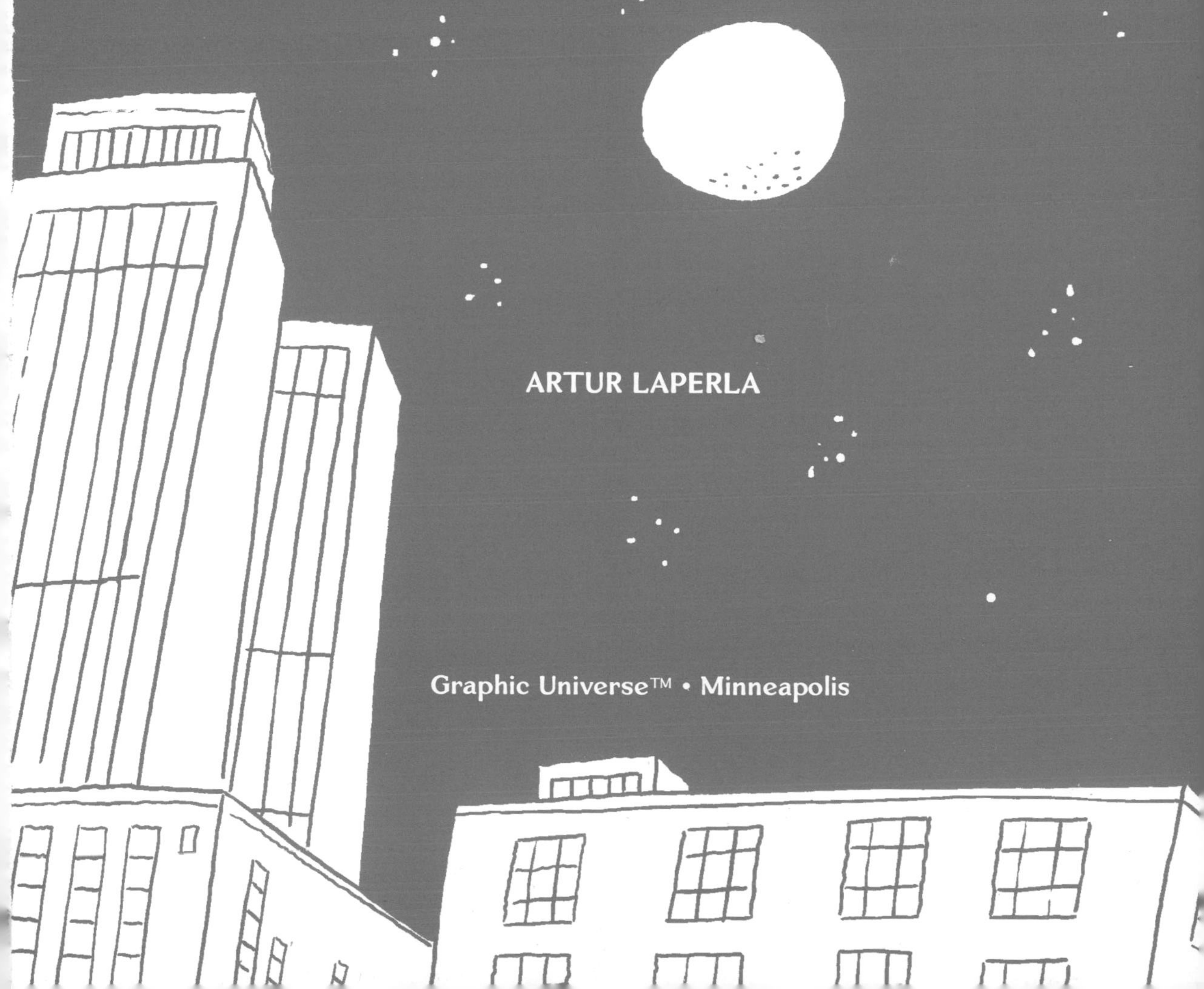

ARTUR LAPERLA

Graphic Universe™ • Minneapolis

Story and illustrations by Artur Laperla
Translation coordinated by Graphic Universe™

First American edition published in 2019 by Graphic Universe™

Graphic Universe™
A division of Lerner Publishing Group, Inc.
241 First Avenue North
Minneapolis, MN 55401 USA

For reading levels and more information, look up this title at www.lernerbooks.com.

Main body text set in CCWildWords 8.5/10. Typeface provided by Comicraft.

Library of Congress Cataloging-in-Publication Data

Names: Laperla (Artist) author, illustrator.
Title: Super Potato's galactic breakout / Artur Laperla.
Description: First American edition. | Minneapolis : Graphic Universe, 2018. | Series: Super
    Potato ; #2 | Summary: "After an evil alien abducts Super Potato, the hero must escape
    from a collection of rare outer-space animals" —Provided by publisher
Identifiers: LCCN 2017043535 (print) | LCCN 2017055590 (ebook) | ISBN 9781541523807 (eb pdf)
    | ISBN 9781512440225 (lb : alk. paper) | ISBN 9781541526464 (pb : alk. paper)
Subjects: LCSH: Graphic novels. | CYAC: Superheroes—Fiction. | Human-alien encounters—
    Fiction. | Potatoes—Fiction. | Humorous stories. | Graphic novels.
Classification: LCC PZ7.7.L367 (ebook) | LCC PZ7.7.L367 Su 2018 (print) | DDC [Fic]—dc23

LC record available at https://lccn.loc.gov/2017043535

Manufactured in the United States of America
4-48026-26141-6/11/2019

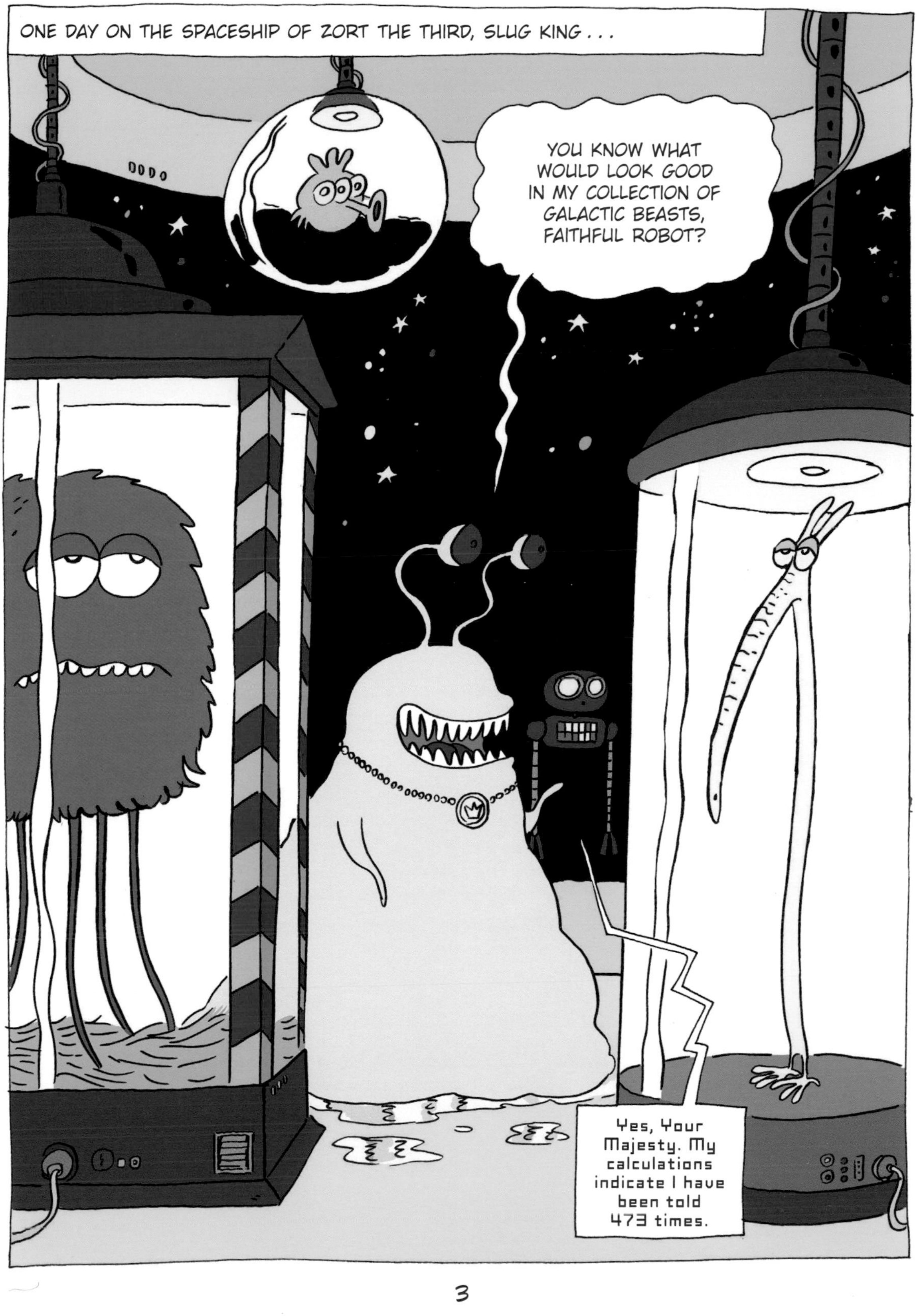

ONE DAY ON THE SPACESHIP OF ZORT THE THIRD, SLUG KING . . .
YOU KNOW WHAT WOULD LOOK GOOD IN MY COLLECTION OF GALACTIC BEASTS, FAITHFUL ROBOT?
Yes, Your Majesty. My calculations indicate I have been told 473 times.

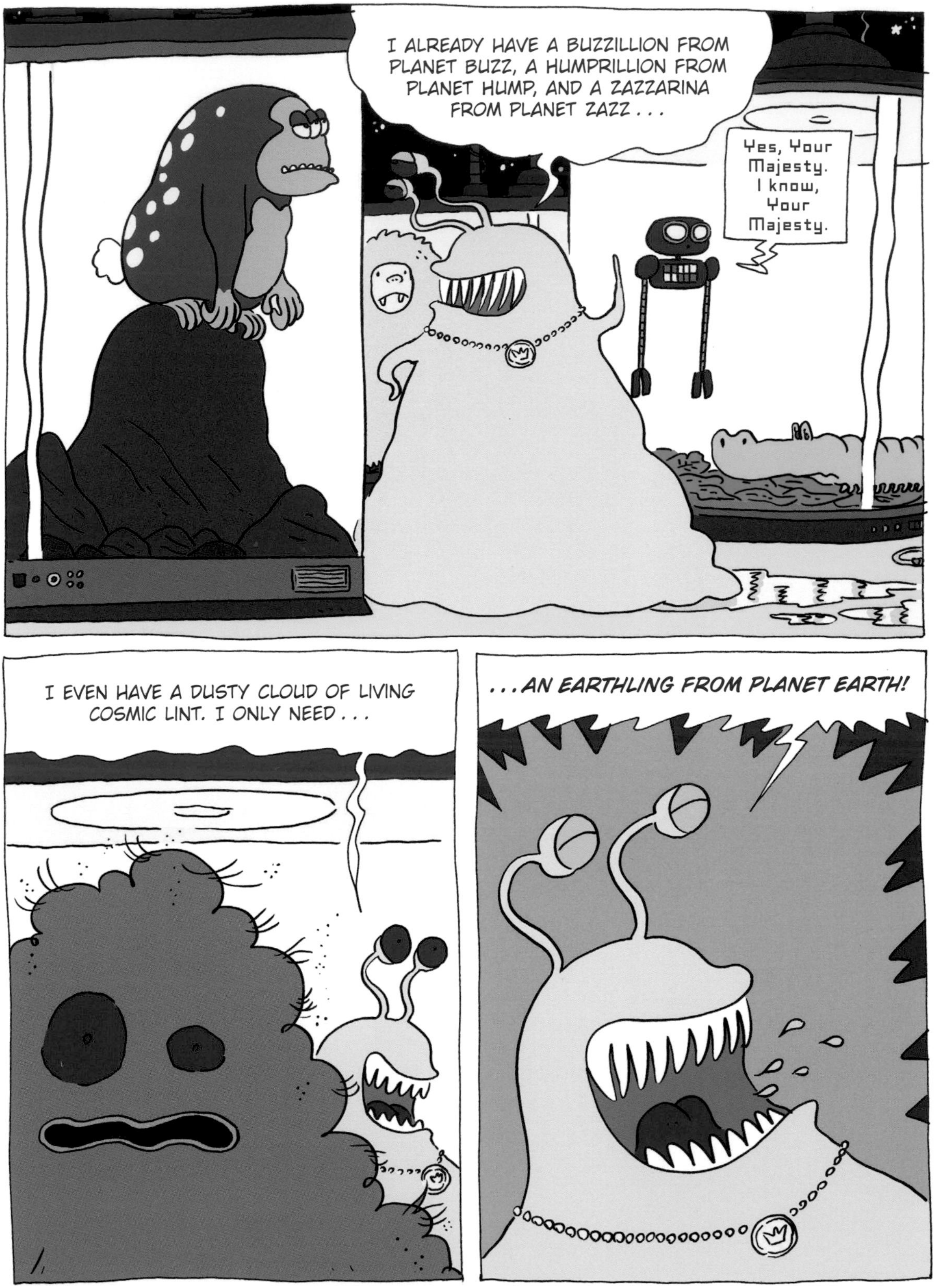
I ALREADY HAVE A BUZZILLION FROM PLANET BUZZ, A HUMPRILLION FROM PLANET HUMP, AND A ZAZZARINA FROM PLANET ZAZZ . . .
Yes, Your Majesty. I know, Your Majesty.
I EVEN HAVE A DUSTY CLOUD OF LIVING COSMIC LINT. I ONLY NEED . . .
. . . AN EARTHLING FROM PLANET EARTH!

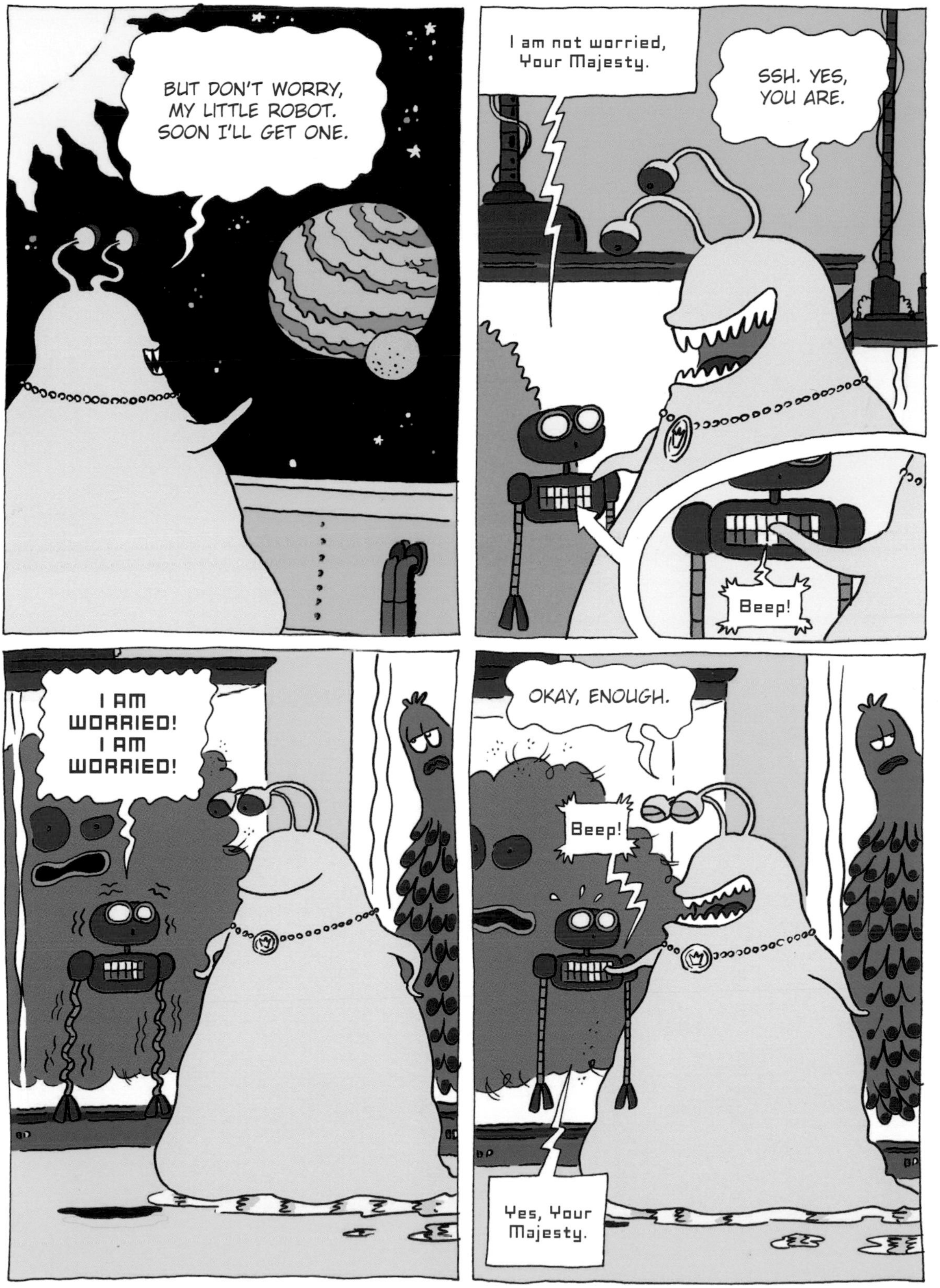

BUT DON'T WORRY, MY LITTLE ROBOT. SOON I'LL GET ONE.
I am not worried, Your Majesty.
SSH. YES, YOU ARE.
Beep!
I AM WORRIED! I AM WORRIED!
OKAY, ENOUGH.
Beep!
Yes, Your Majesty.

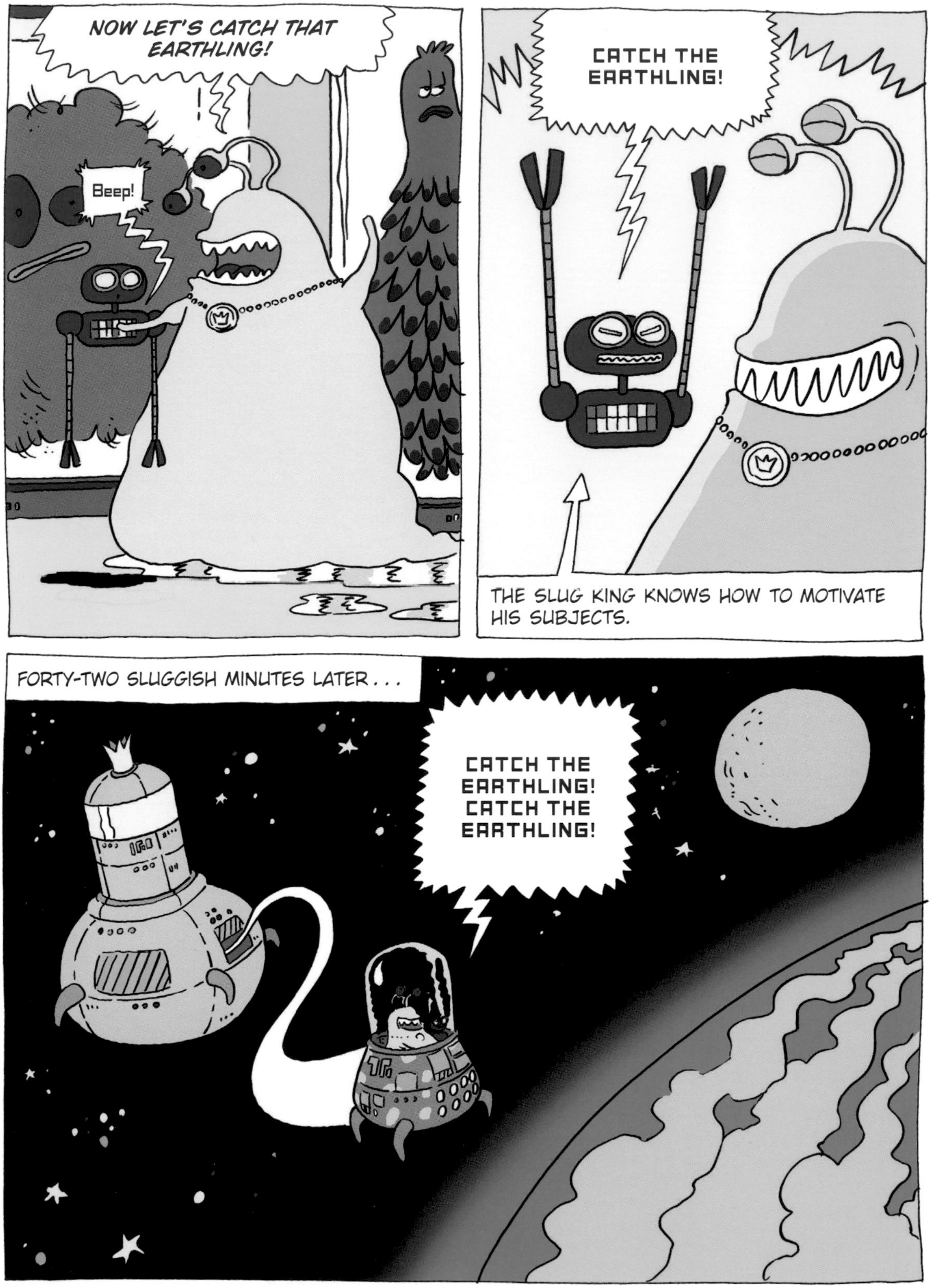
NOW LET'S CATCH THAT EARTHLING!
Beep!
CATCH THE EARTHLING!
THE SLUG KING KNOWS HOW TO MOTIVATE HIS SUBJECTS.
FORTY-TWO SLUGGISH MINUTES LATER . . .
CATCH THE EARTHLING! CATCH THE EARTHLING!

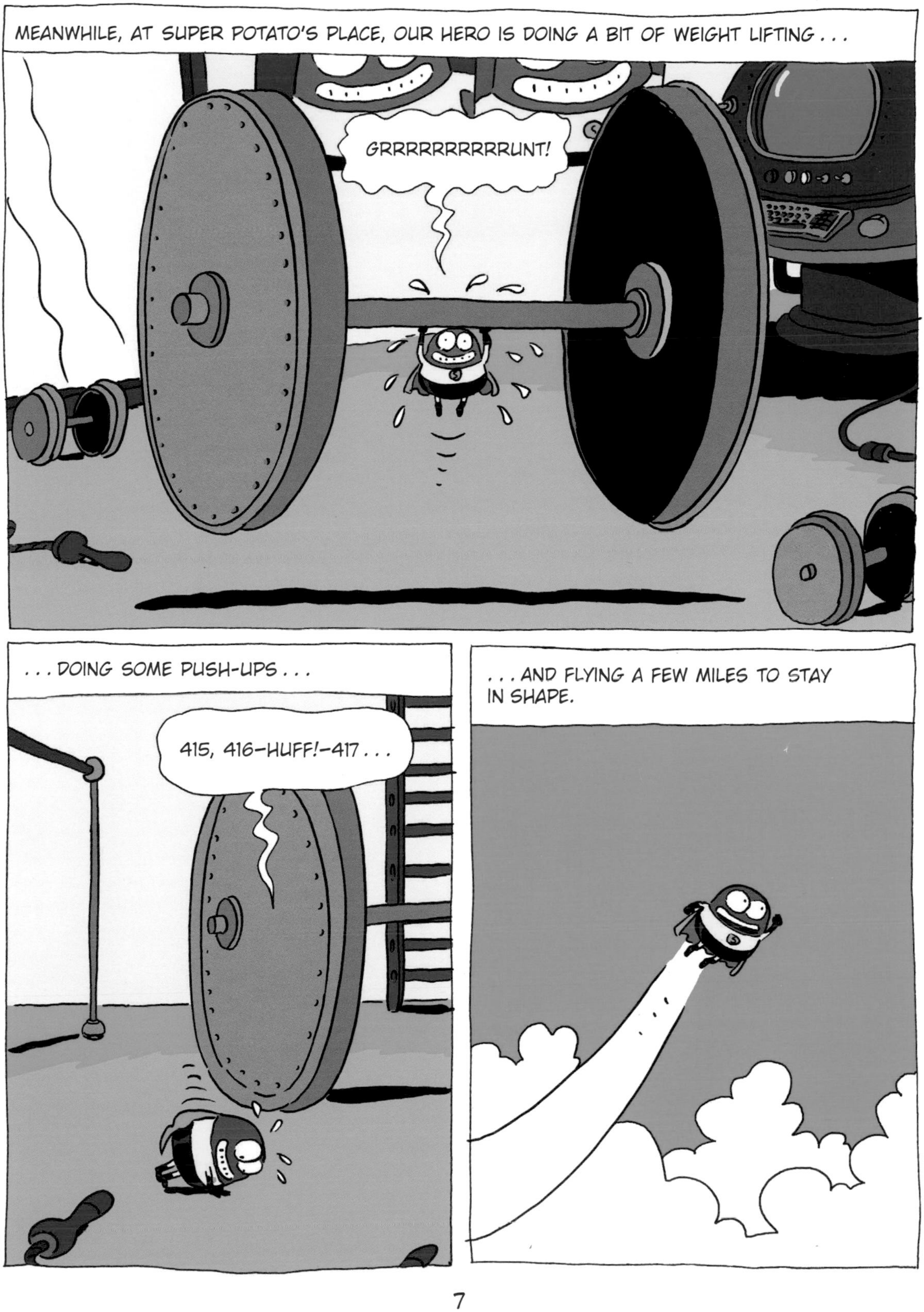
MEANWHILE, AT SUPER POTATO'S PLACE, OUR HERO IS DOING A BIT OF WEIGHT LIFTING . . .
GRRRRRRRRRRUNT!
. . . DOING SOME PUSH-UPS . . .
415, 416–HUFF!–417 . . .
. . . AND FLYING A FEW MILES TO STAY IN SHAPE.

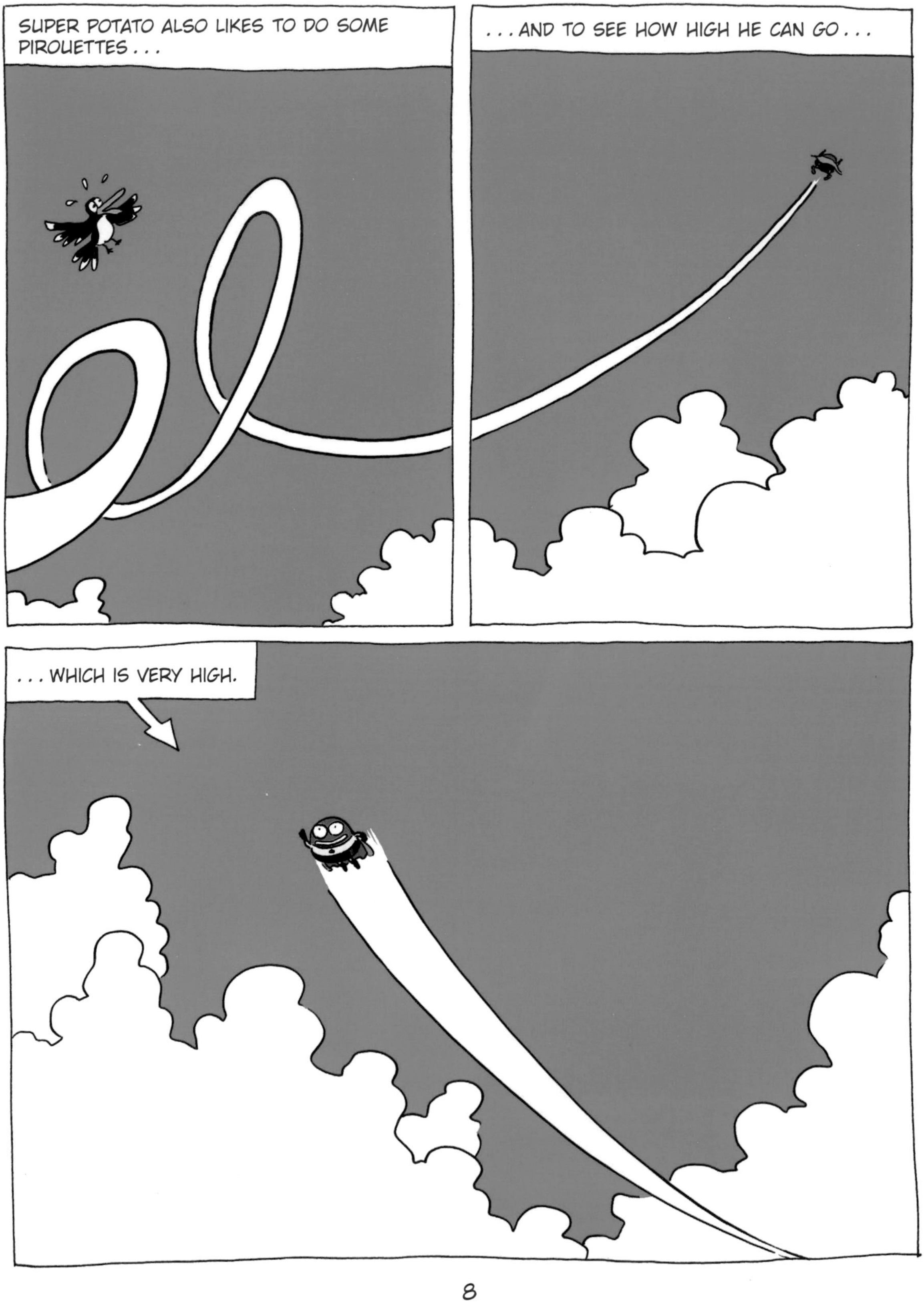
SUPER POTATO ALSO LIKES TO DO SOME PIROUETTES . . .
. . . AND TO SEE HOW HIGH HE CAN GO . . .
. . . WHICH IS VERY HIGH.

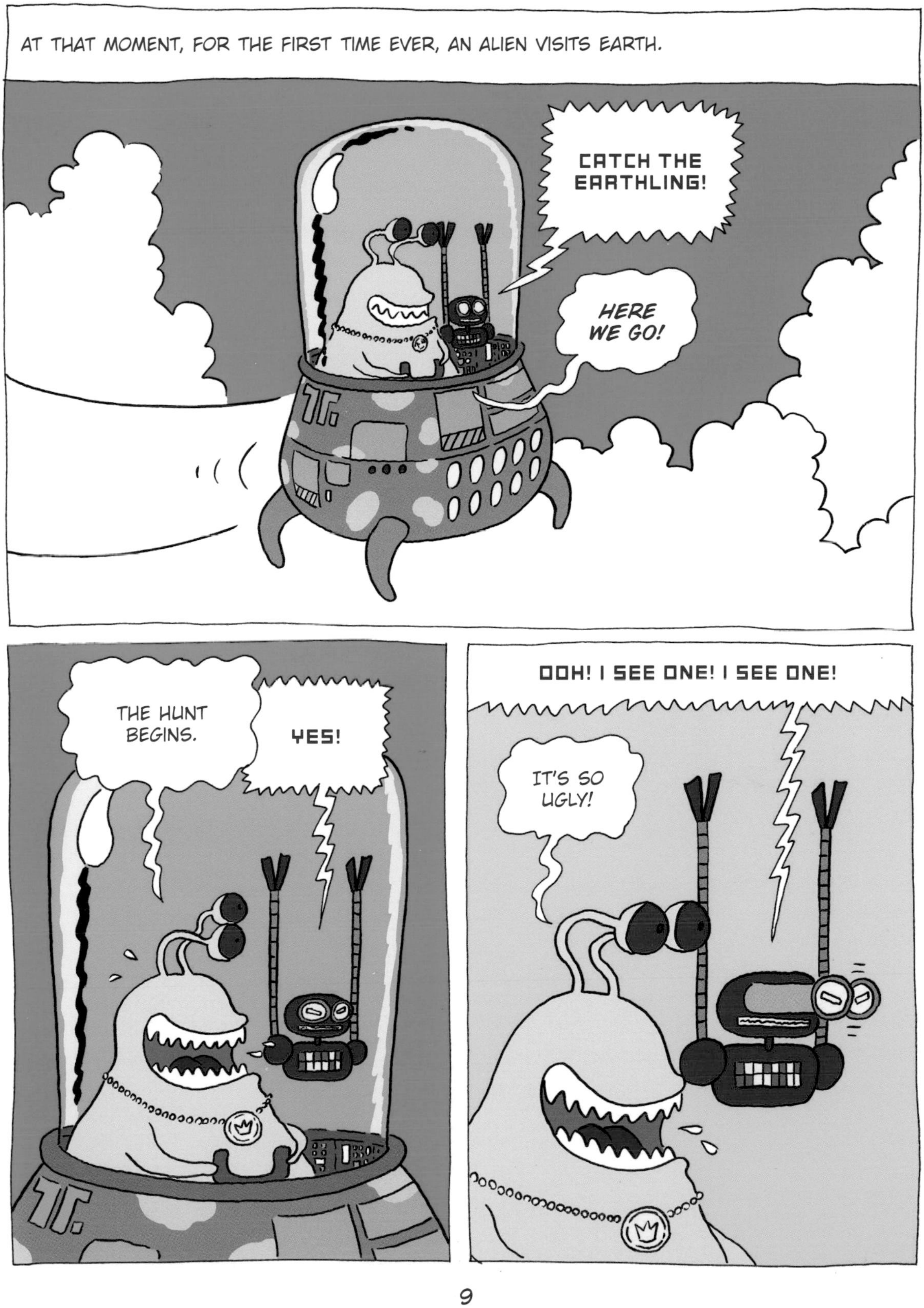
AT THAT MOMENT, FOR THE FIRST TIME EVER, AN ALIEN VISITS EARTH.
CATCH THE EARTHLING!
HERE WE GO!
THE HUNT BEGINS.
YES!
OOH! I SEE ONE! I SEE ONE!
IT'S SO UGLY!

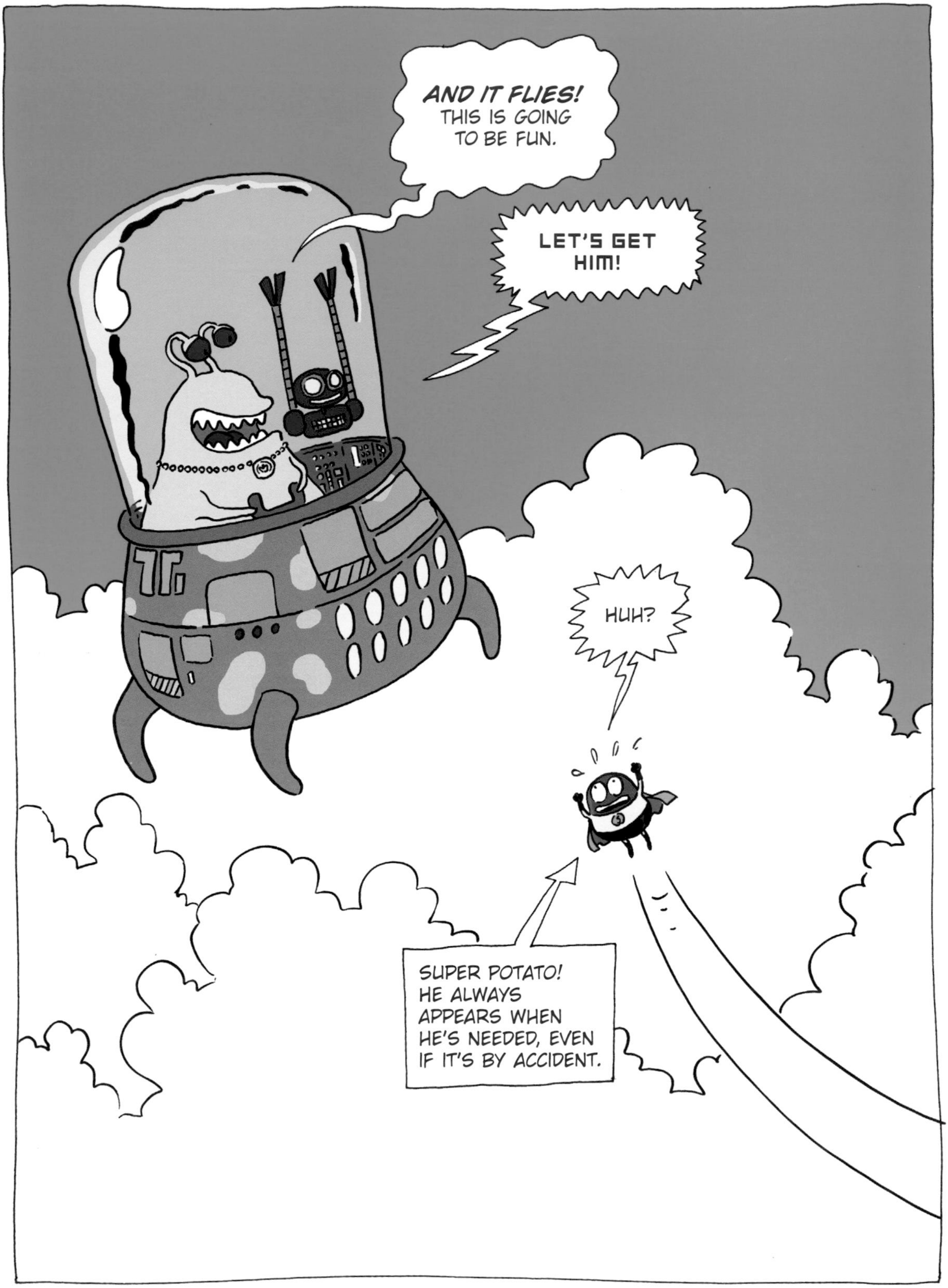

AND IT FLIES! THIS IS GOING TO BE FUN.
LET'S GET HIM!
HUH?
SUPER POTATO! HE ALWAYS APPEARS WHEN HE'S NEEDED, EVEN IF IT'S BY ACCIDENT.

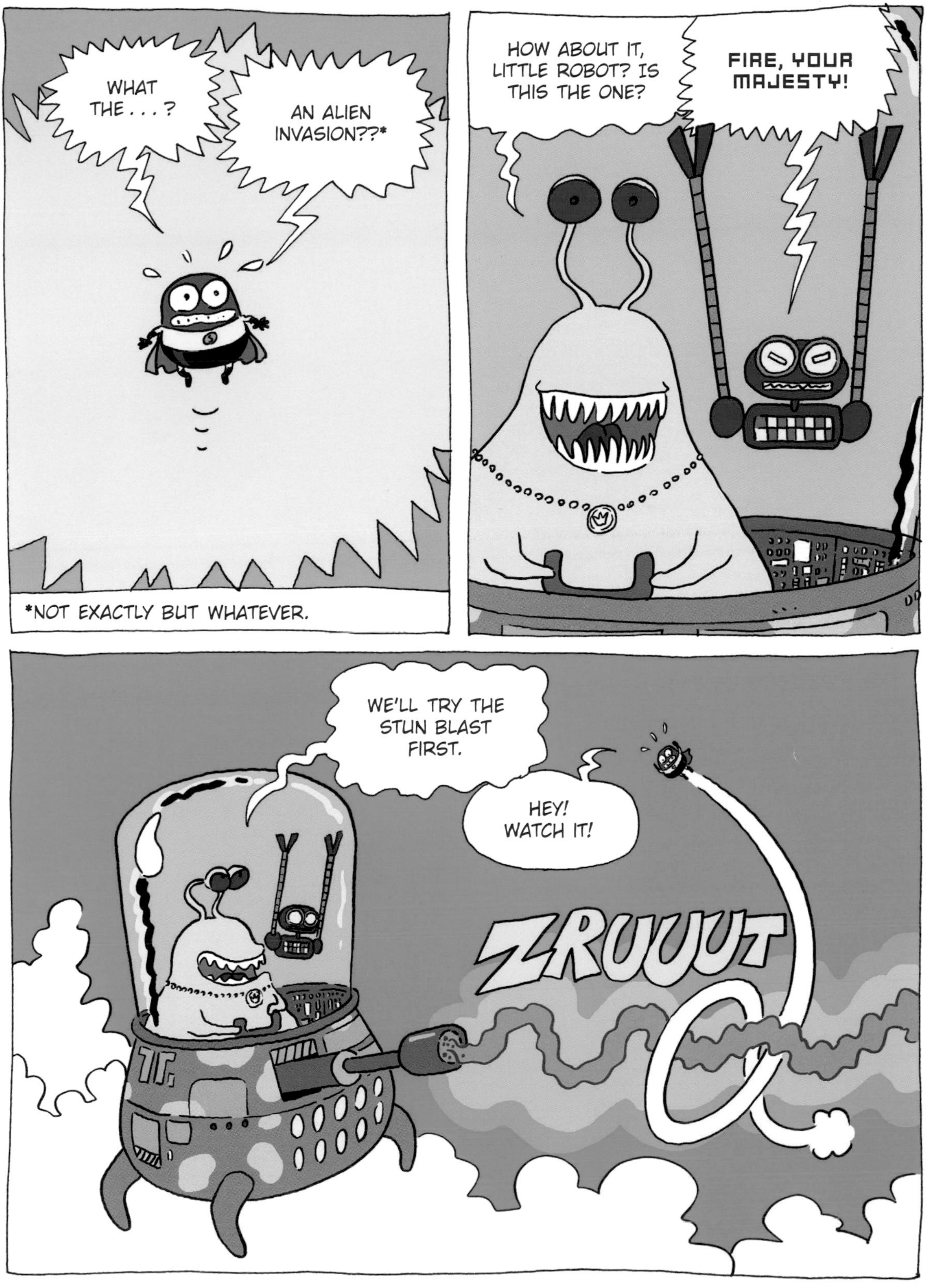
WHAT THE . . . ?
AN ALIEN INVASION??*
*NOT EXACTLY BUT WHATEVER.
HOW ABOUT IT, LITTLE ROBOT? IS THIS THE ONE?
FIRE, YOUR MAJESTY!
WE'LL TRY THE STUN BLAST FIRST.
HEY! WATCH IT!
ZRUUUT

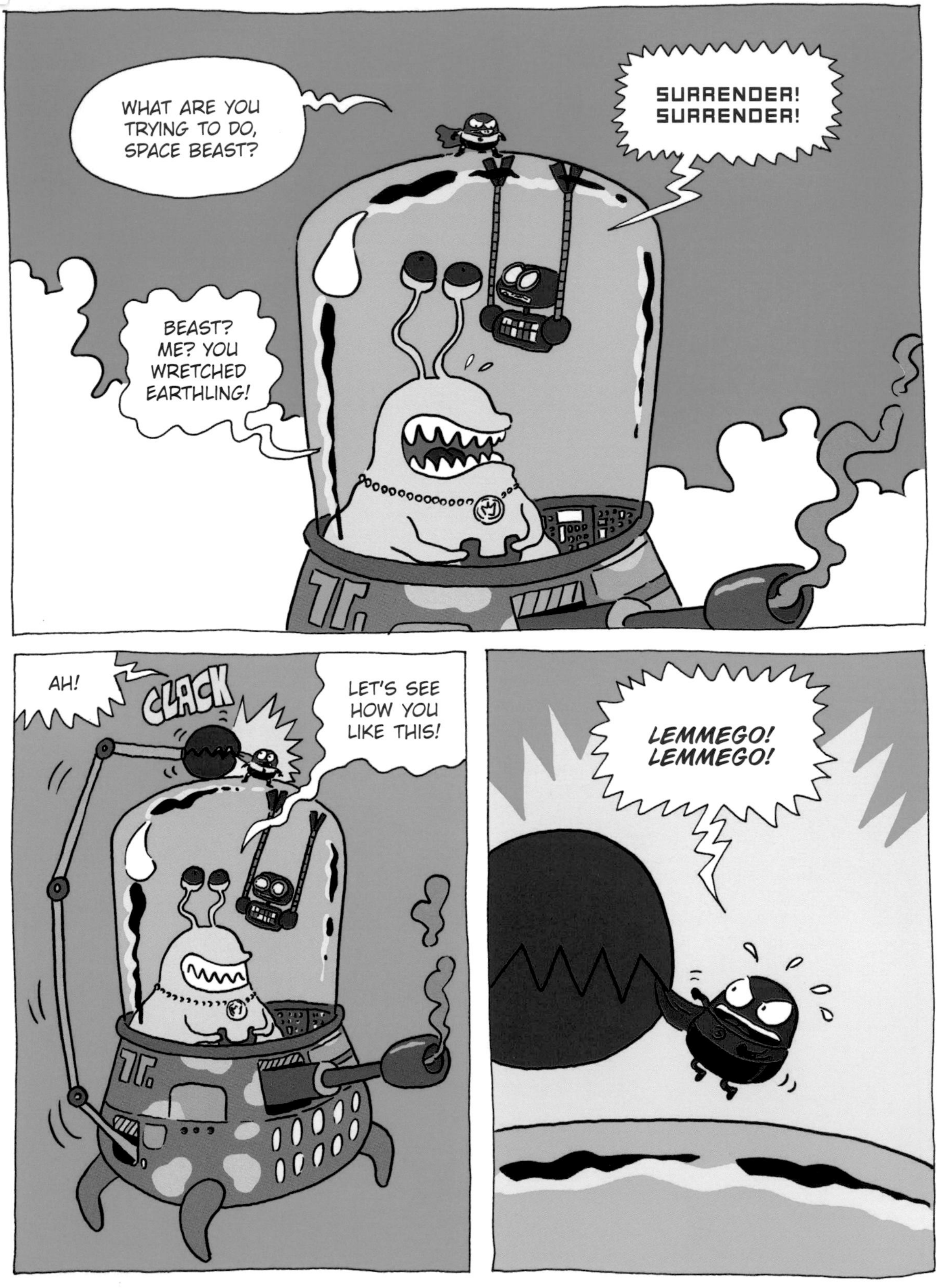
WHAT ARE YOU TRYING TO DO, SPACE BEAST?
SURRENDER! SURRENDER!
BEAST? ME? YOU WRETCHED EARTHLING!
AH!
CLACK
LET'S SEE HOW YOU LIKE THIS!
LEMMEGO! LEMMEGO!

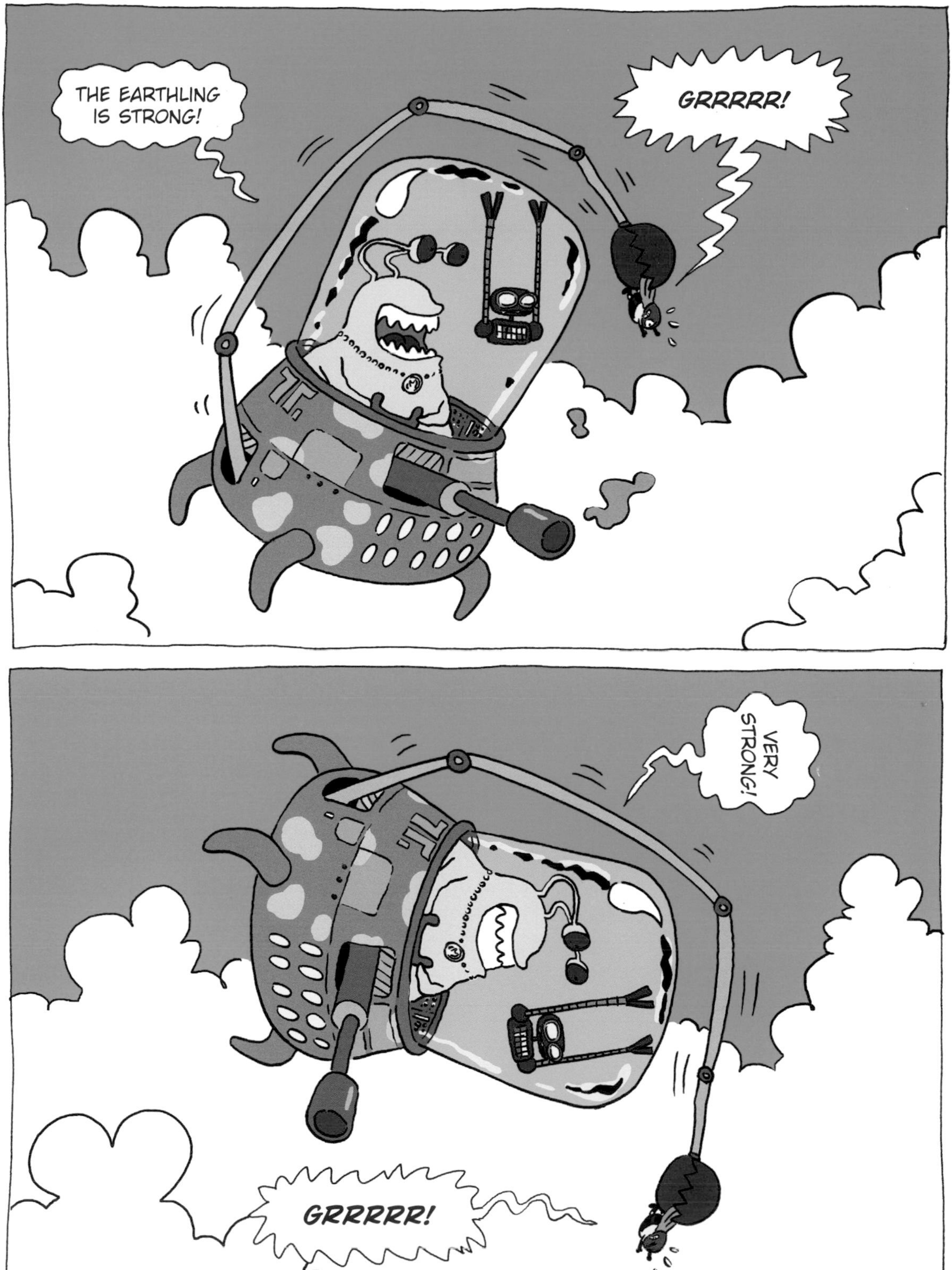
THE EARTHLING IS STRONG!
GRRRRR!
VERY STRONG!
GRRRRR!

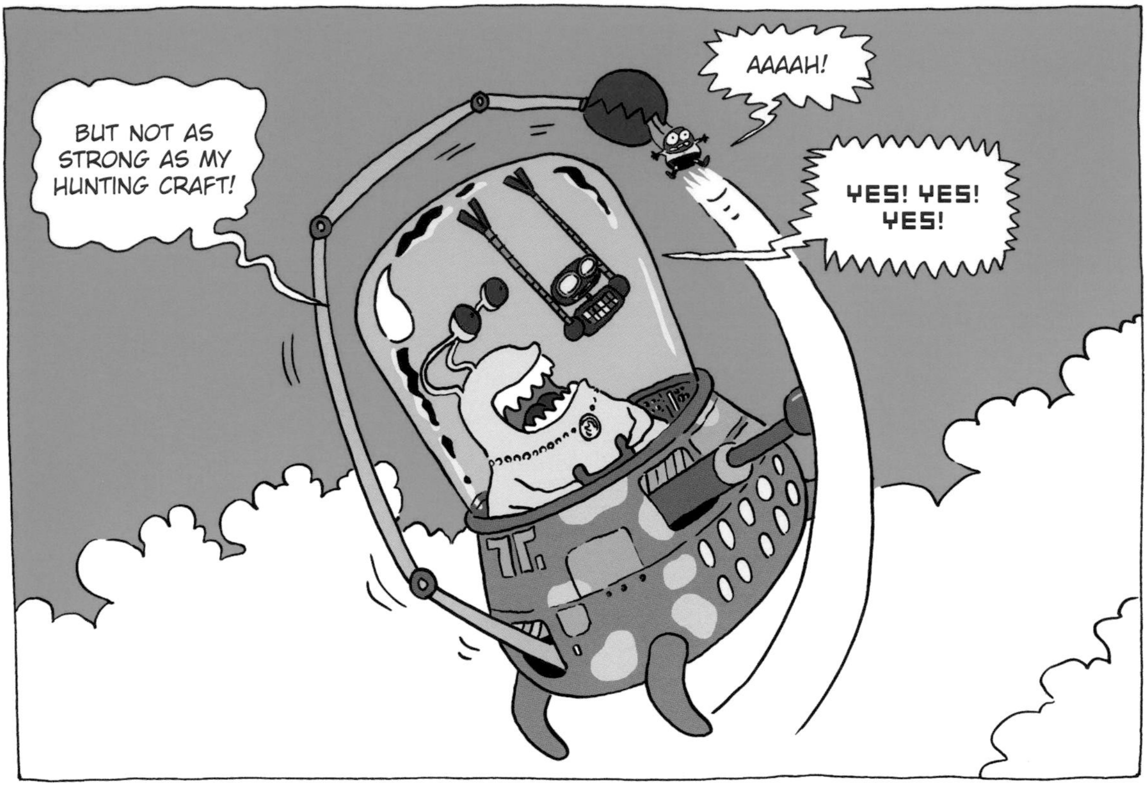
BUT NOT AS STRONG AS MY HUNTING CRAFT!
AAAAH!
YES! YES! YES!

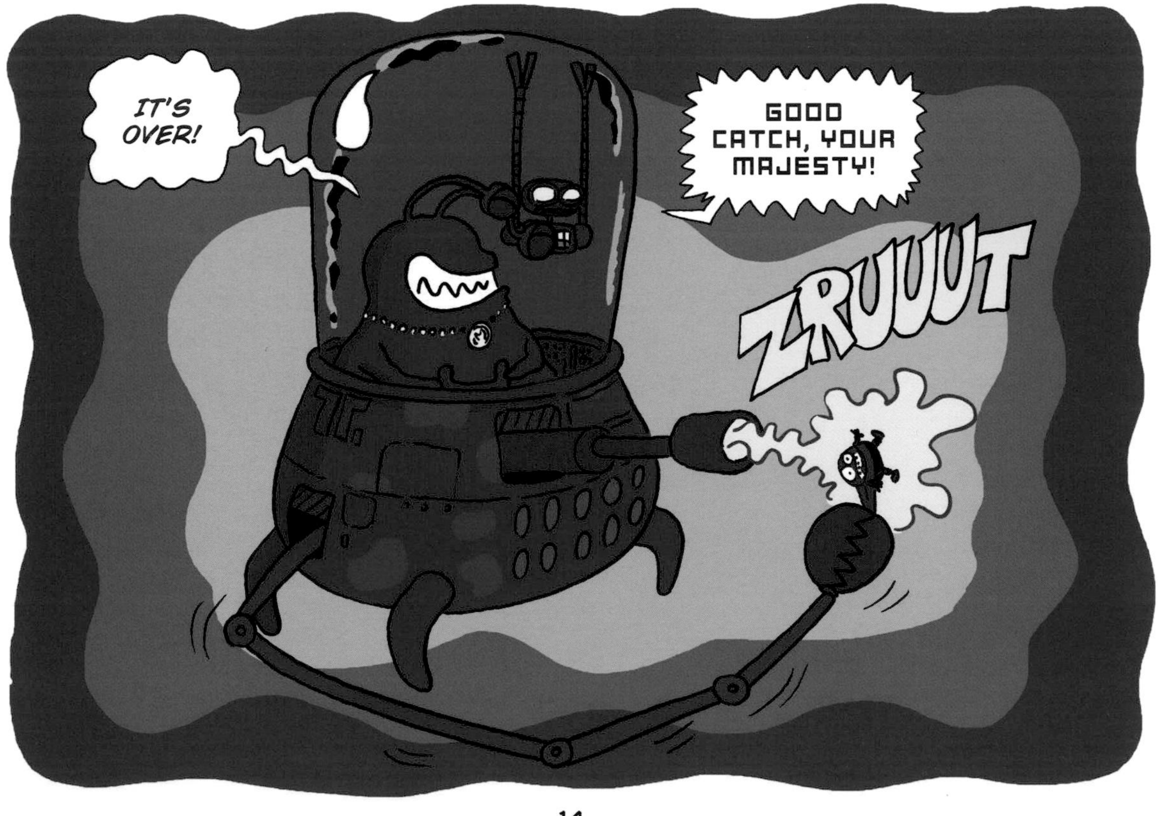
IT'S OVER!
GOOD CATCH, YOUR MAJESTY!
ZRUUUT

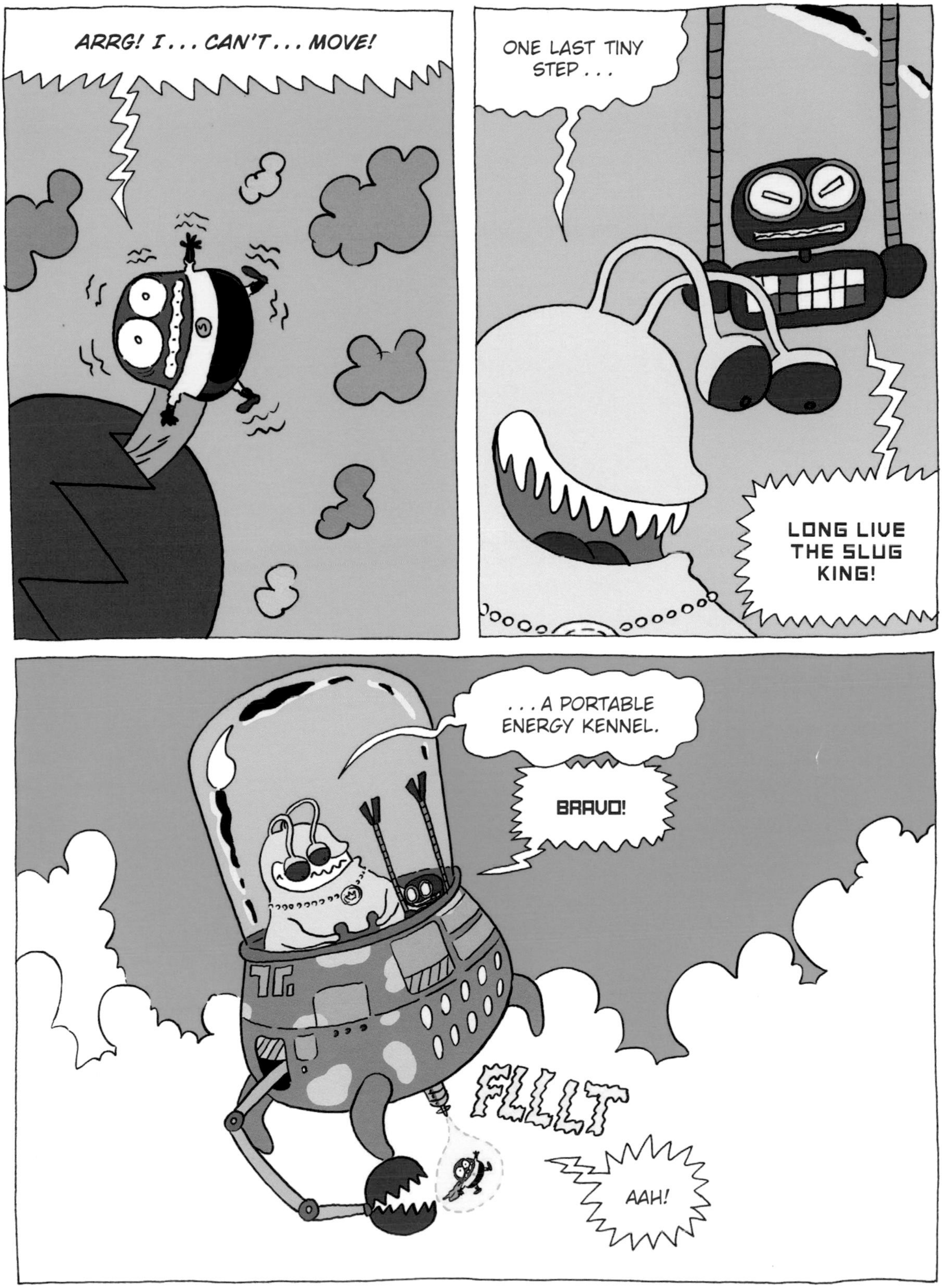
ARRG! I . . . CAN'T . . . MOVE!
ONE LAST TINY STEP . . .
LONG LIVE THE SLUG KING!
. . . A PORTABLE ENERGY KENNEL.
BRAVO!
FLLLT
AAH!

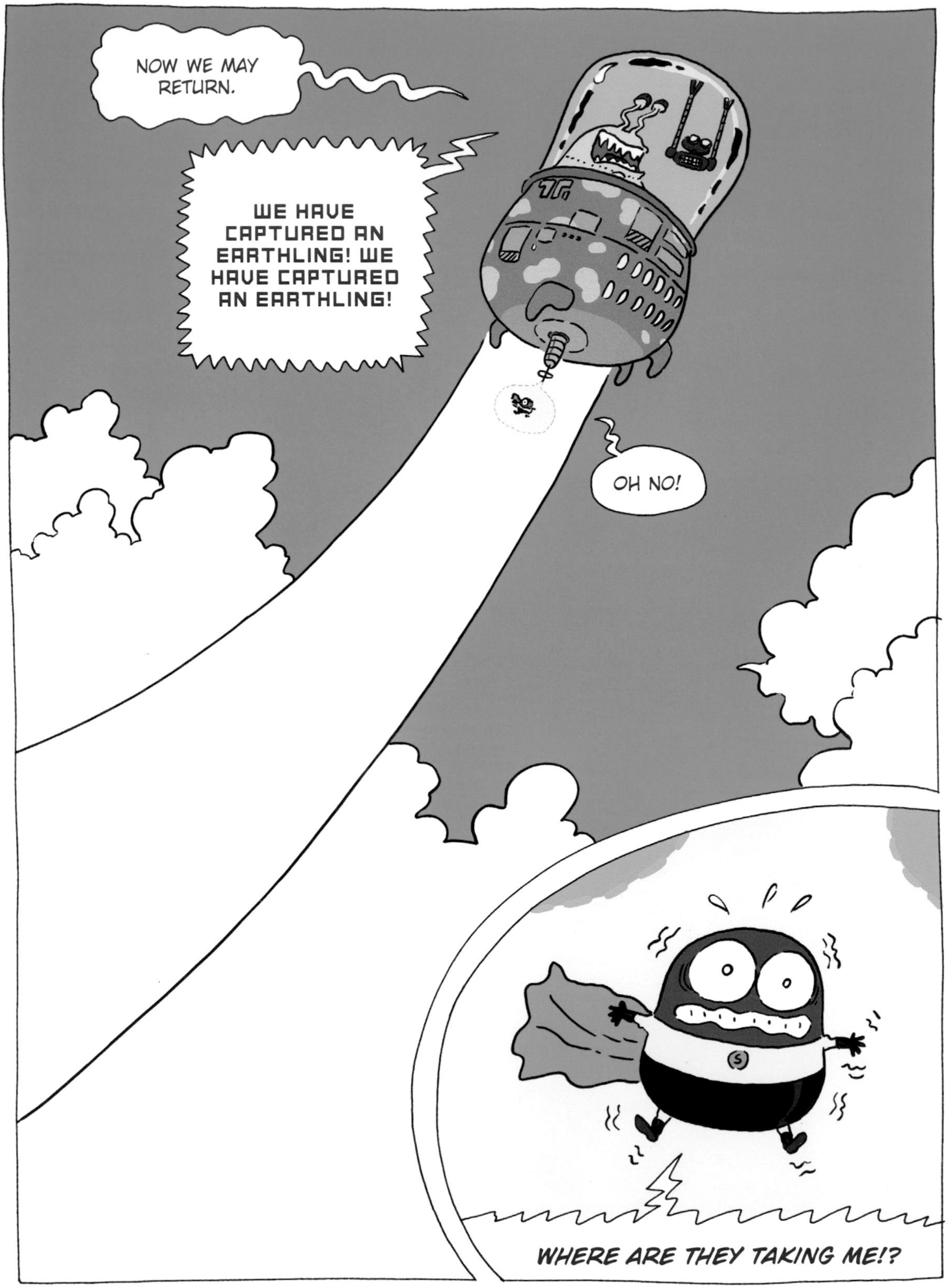
NOW WE MAY RETURN.
WE HAVE CAPTURED AN EARTHLING! WE HAVE CAPTURED AN EARTHLING!
OH NO!
WHERE ARE THEY TAKING ME!?

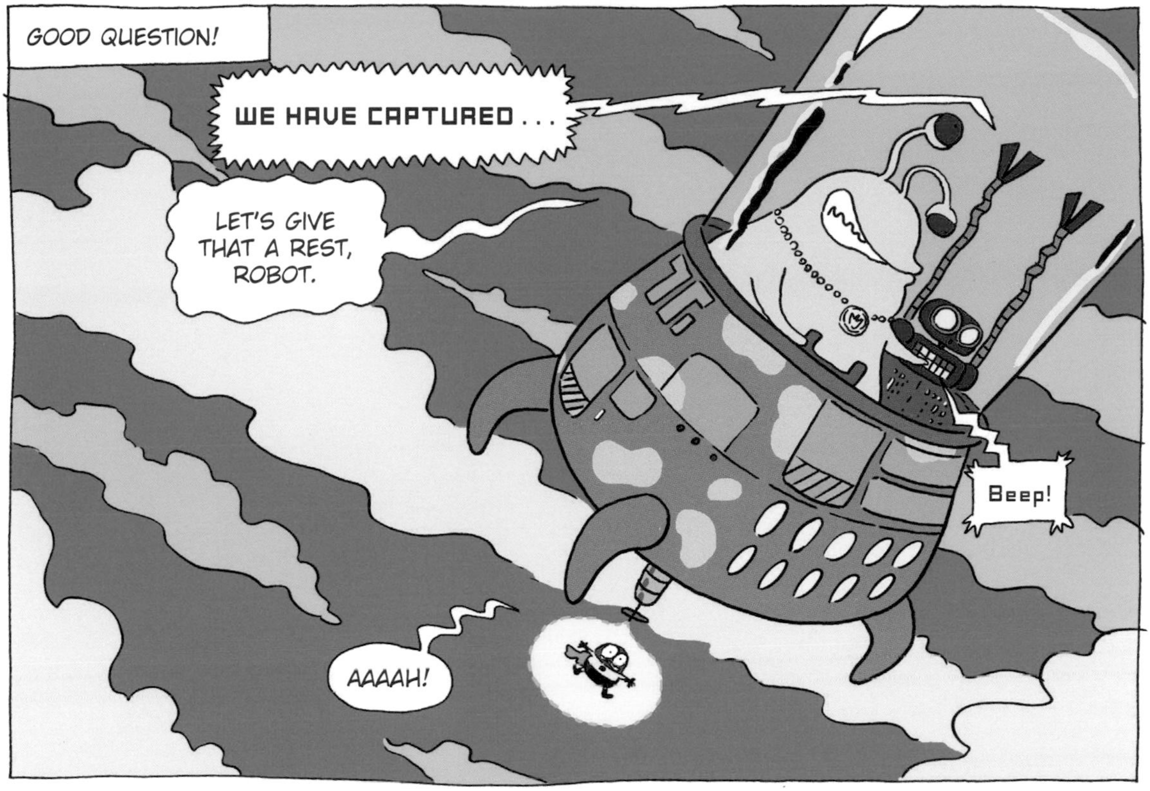
GOOD QUESTION!
WE HAVE CAPTURED . . .
LET'S GIVE THAT A REST, ROBOT.
Beep!
AAAAH!

THE HUNTING CRAFT, OF COURSE, IS HEADED FOR THE DREADED ROYAL SHIP OF THE SLUG KING.

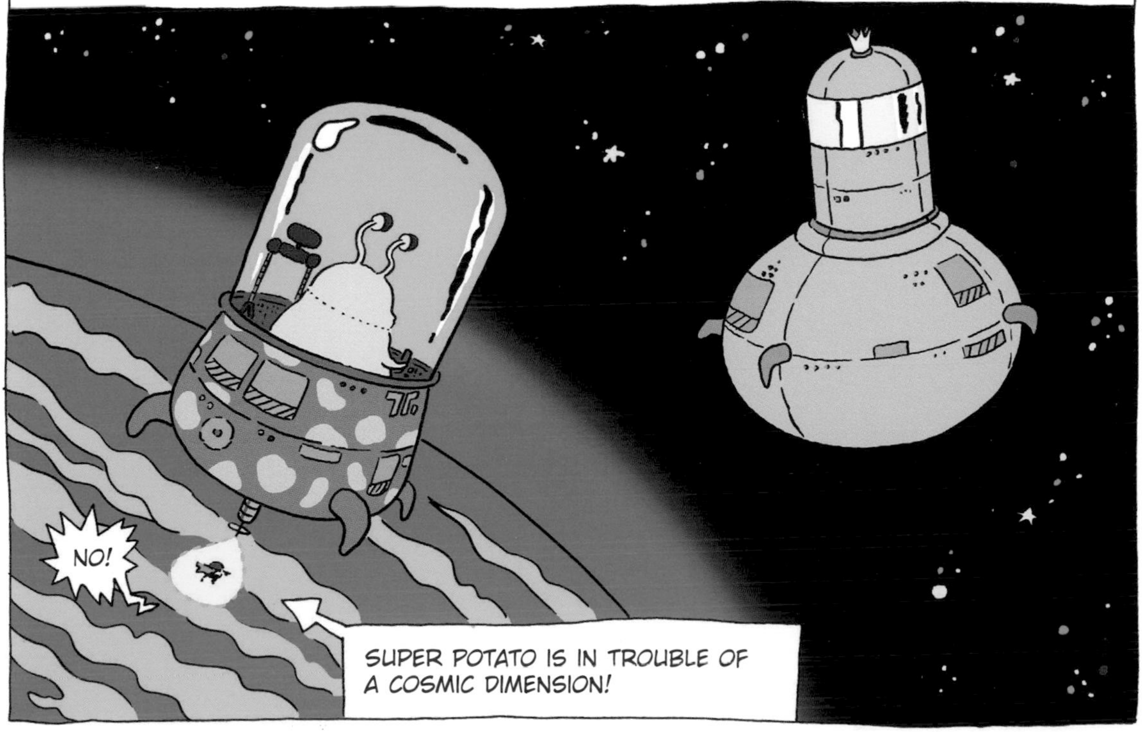
NO!
SUPER POTATO IS IN TROUBLE OF A COSMIC DIMENSION!

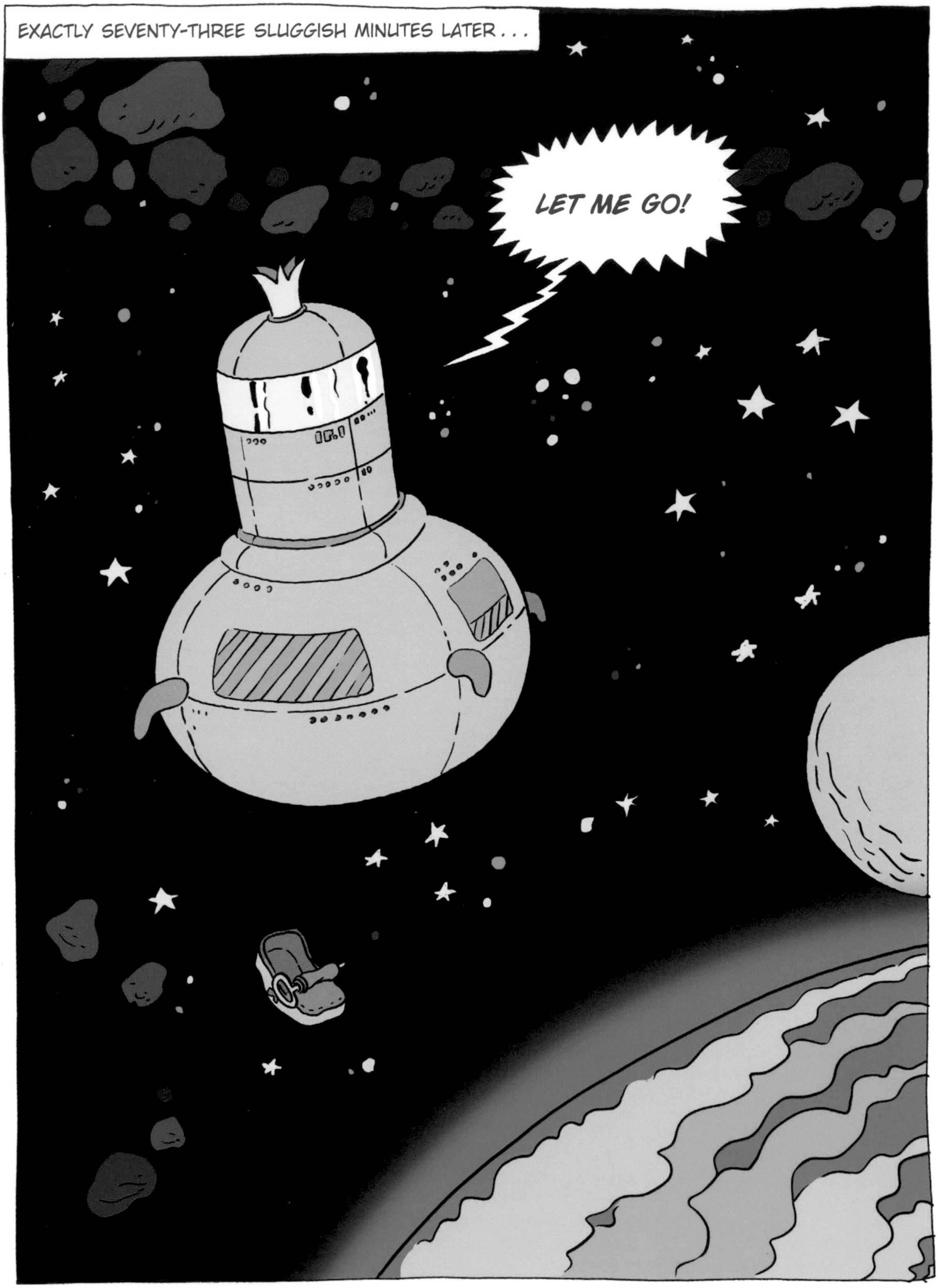
EXACTLY SEVENTY-THREE SLUGGISH MINUTES LATER . . .
LET ME GO!

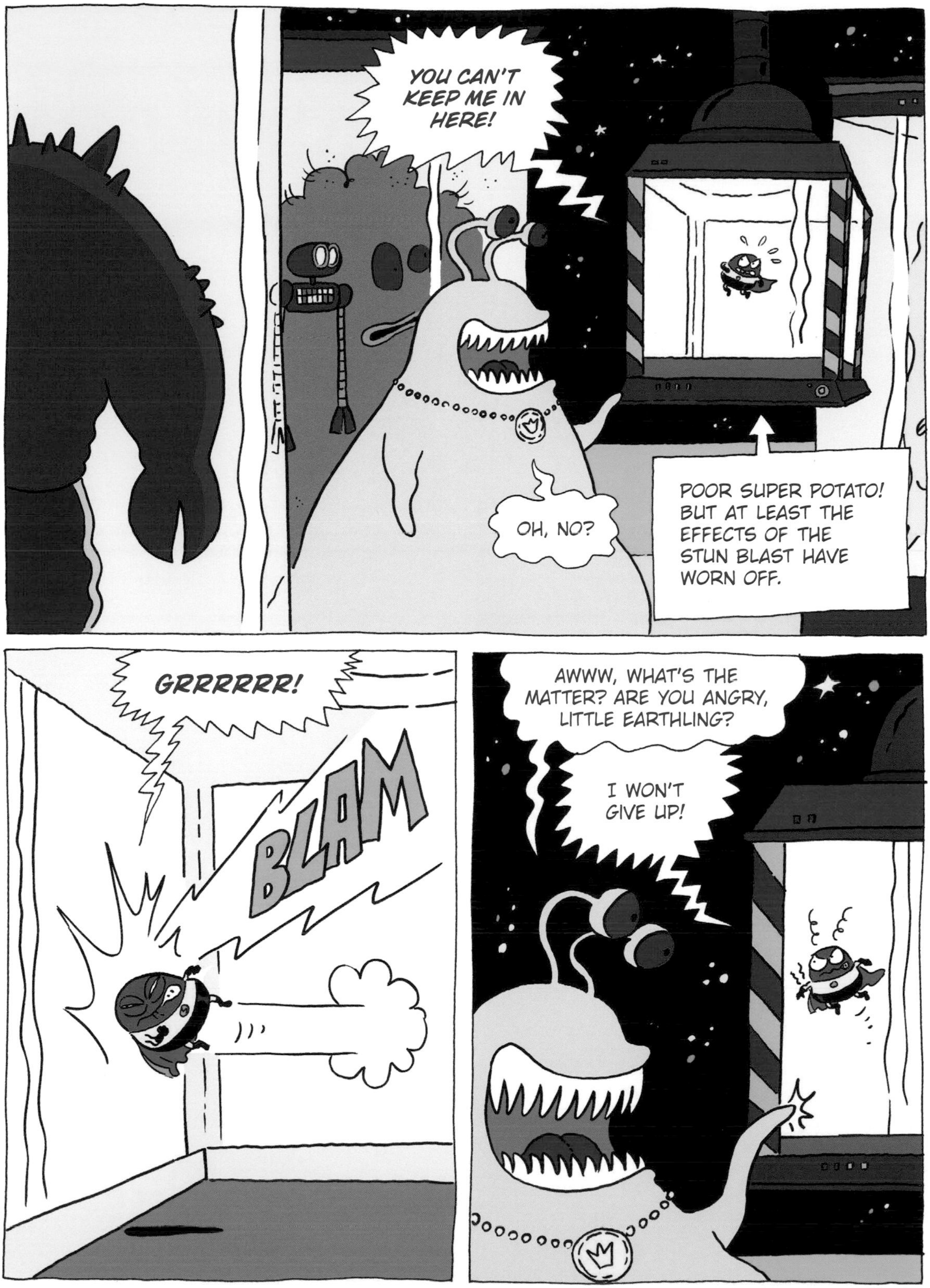
YOU CAN'T KEEP ME IN HERE!
OH, NO?
POOR SUPER POTATO! BUT AT LEAST THE EFFECTS OF THE STUN BLAST HAVE WORN OFF.
GRRRRRR!
BLAM
AWWW, WHAT'S THE MATTER? ARE YOU ANGRY, LITTLE EARTHLING?
I WON'T GIVE UP!

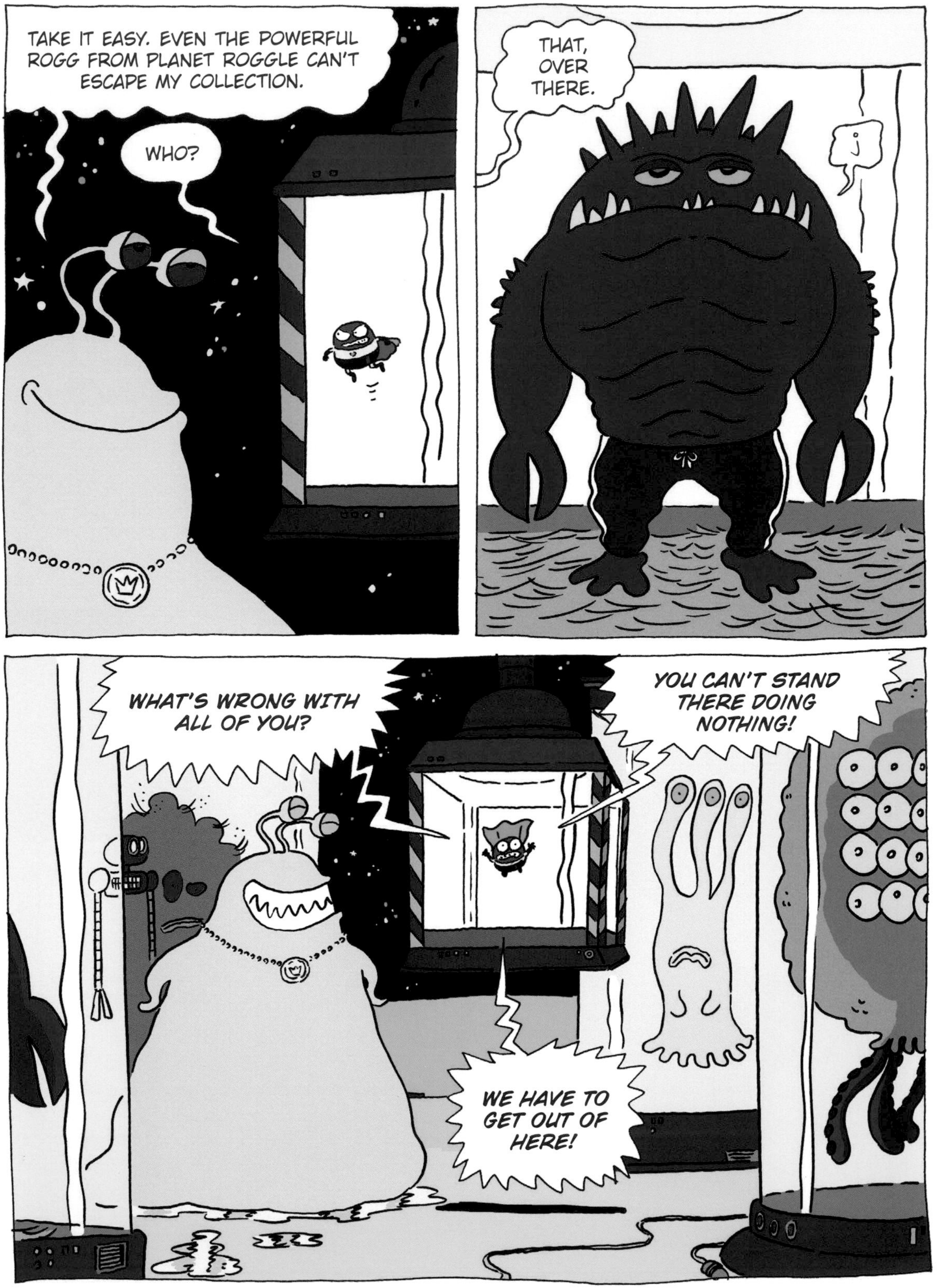
TAKE IT EASY. EVEN THE POWERFUL ROGG FROM PLANET ROGGLE CAN'T ESCAPE MY COLLECTION.
WHO?
THAT, OVER THERE.
¡
WHAT'S WRONG WITH ALL OF YOU?
YOU CAN'T STAND THERE DOING NOTHING!
WE HAVE TO GET OUT OF HERE!

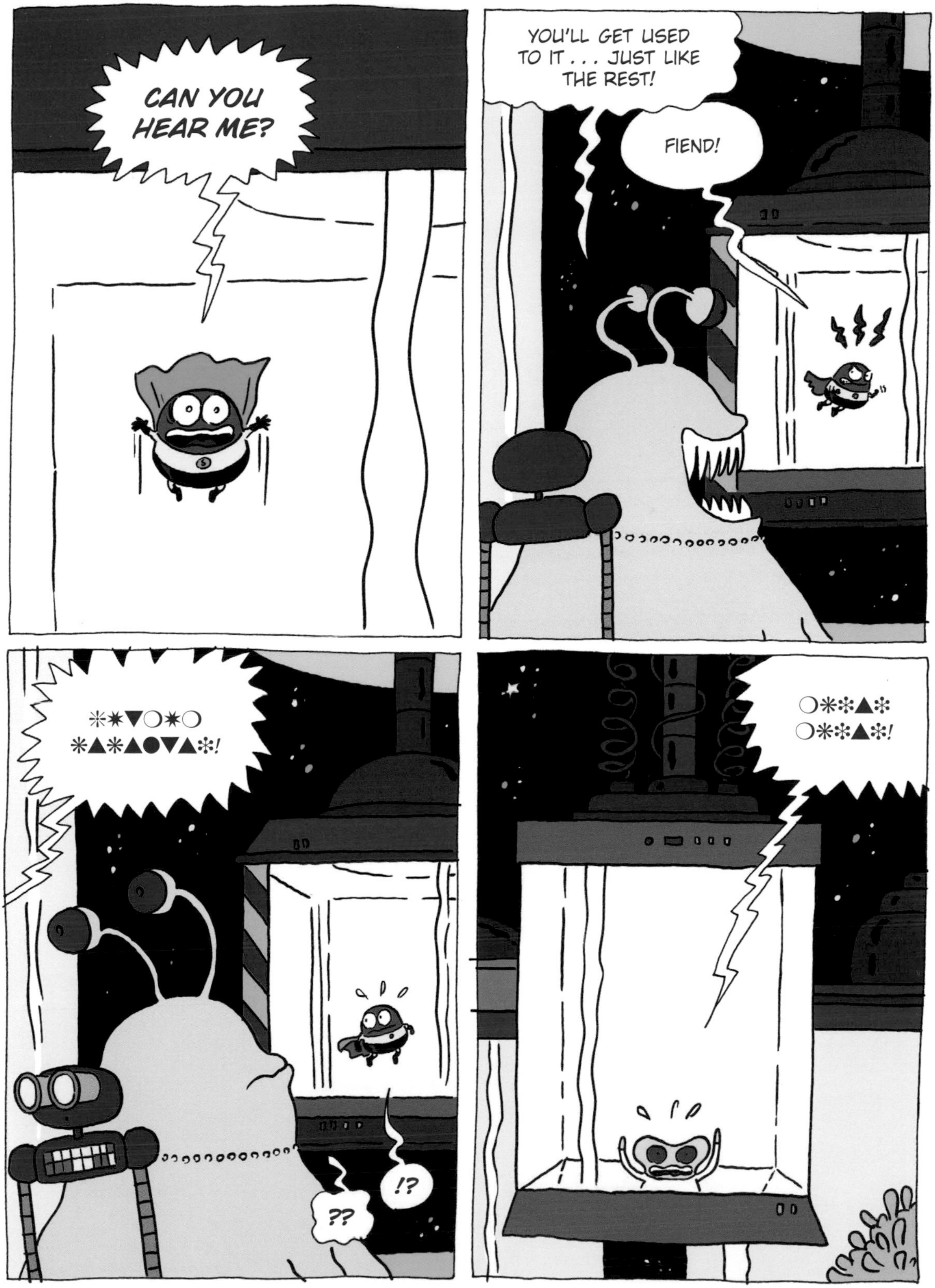
CAN YOU HEAR ME?
YOU'LL GET USED TO IT . . . JUST LIKE THE REST!
FIEND!
!?
??

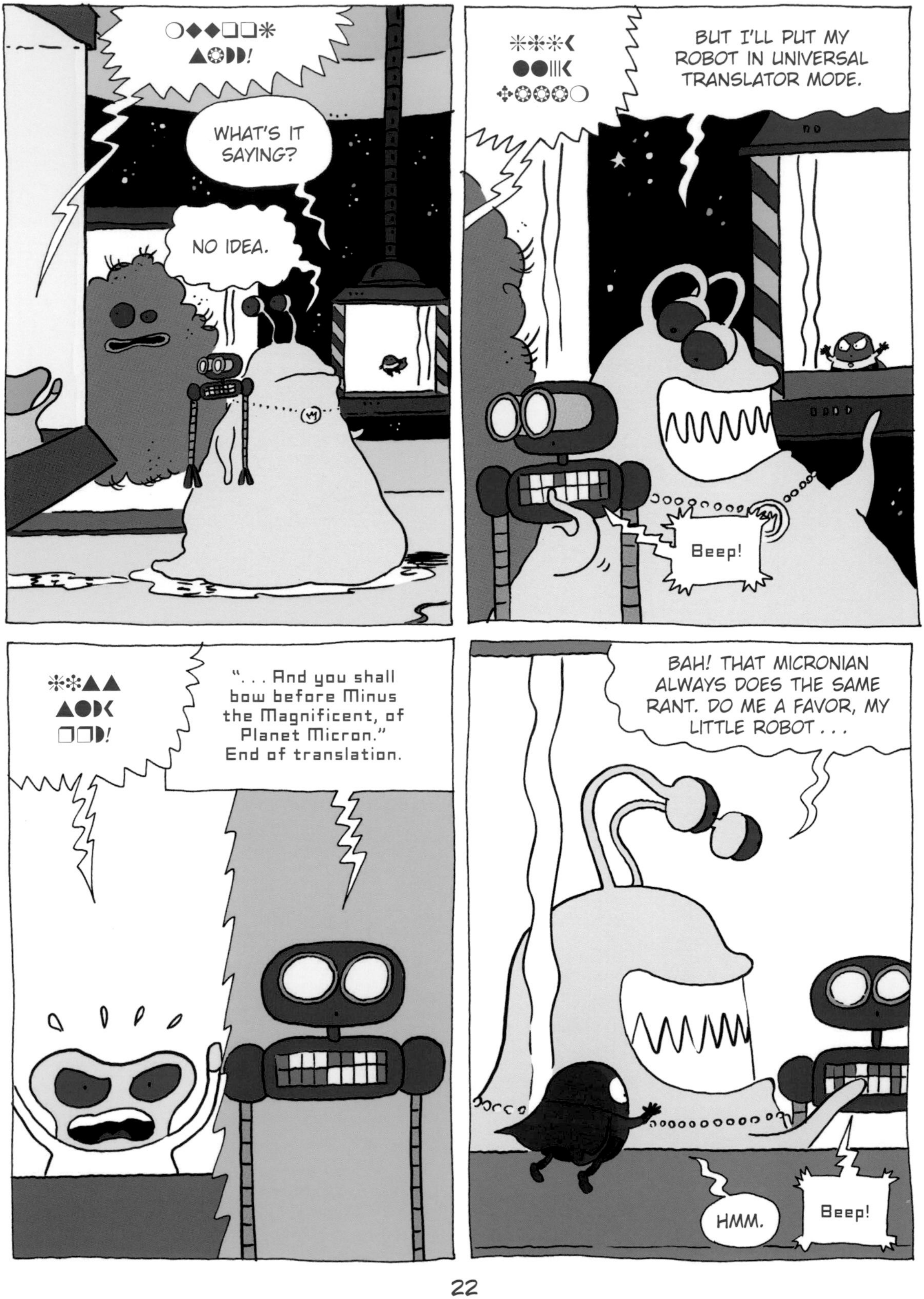
WHAT'S IT SAYING?
NO IDEA.
BUT I'LL PUT MY ROBOT IN UNIVERSAL TRANSLATOR MODE.
Beep!
". . . And you shall bow before Minus the Magnificent, of Planet Micron." End of translation.
BAH! THAT MICRONIAN ALWAYS DOES THE SAME RANT. DO ME A FAVOR, MY LITTLE ROBOT . . .
HMM.
Beep!

...CLEAN UP IN HERE WHILE I TAKE MY NAP.

Yes, Your Majesty.

THE SIGHT OF THE SLUG KING NAPPING ISN'T VERY INTERESTING...

ZZZZZZZZZZZZ

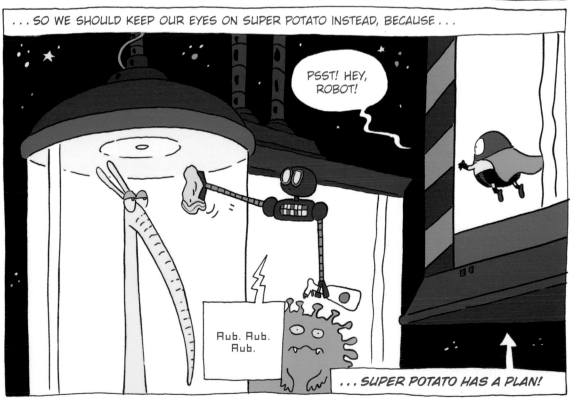

...SO WE SHOULD KEEP OUR EYES ON SUPER POTATO INSTEAD, BECAUSE...

PSST! HEY, ROBOT!

Rub. Rub. Rub.

...SUPER POTATO HAS A PLAN!

23

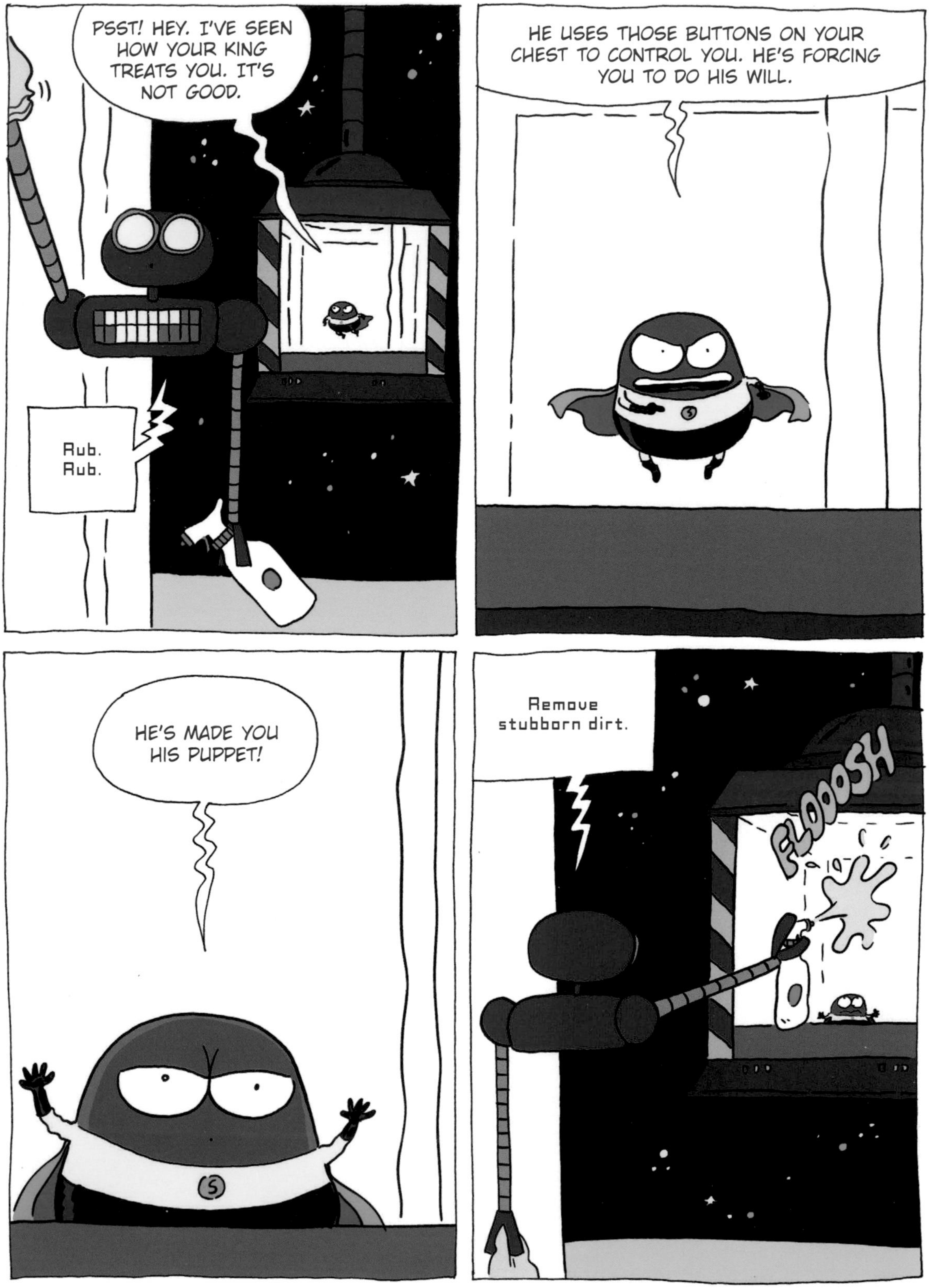
PSST! HEY. I'VE SEEN HOW YOUR KING TREATS YOU. IT'S NOT GOOD.
Rub. Rub.
HE USES THOSE BUTTONS ON YOUR CHEST TO CONTROL YOU. HE'S FORCING YOU TO DO HIS WILL.
HE'S MADE YOU HIS PUPPET!
Remove stubborn dirt.
FLOOSH

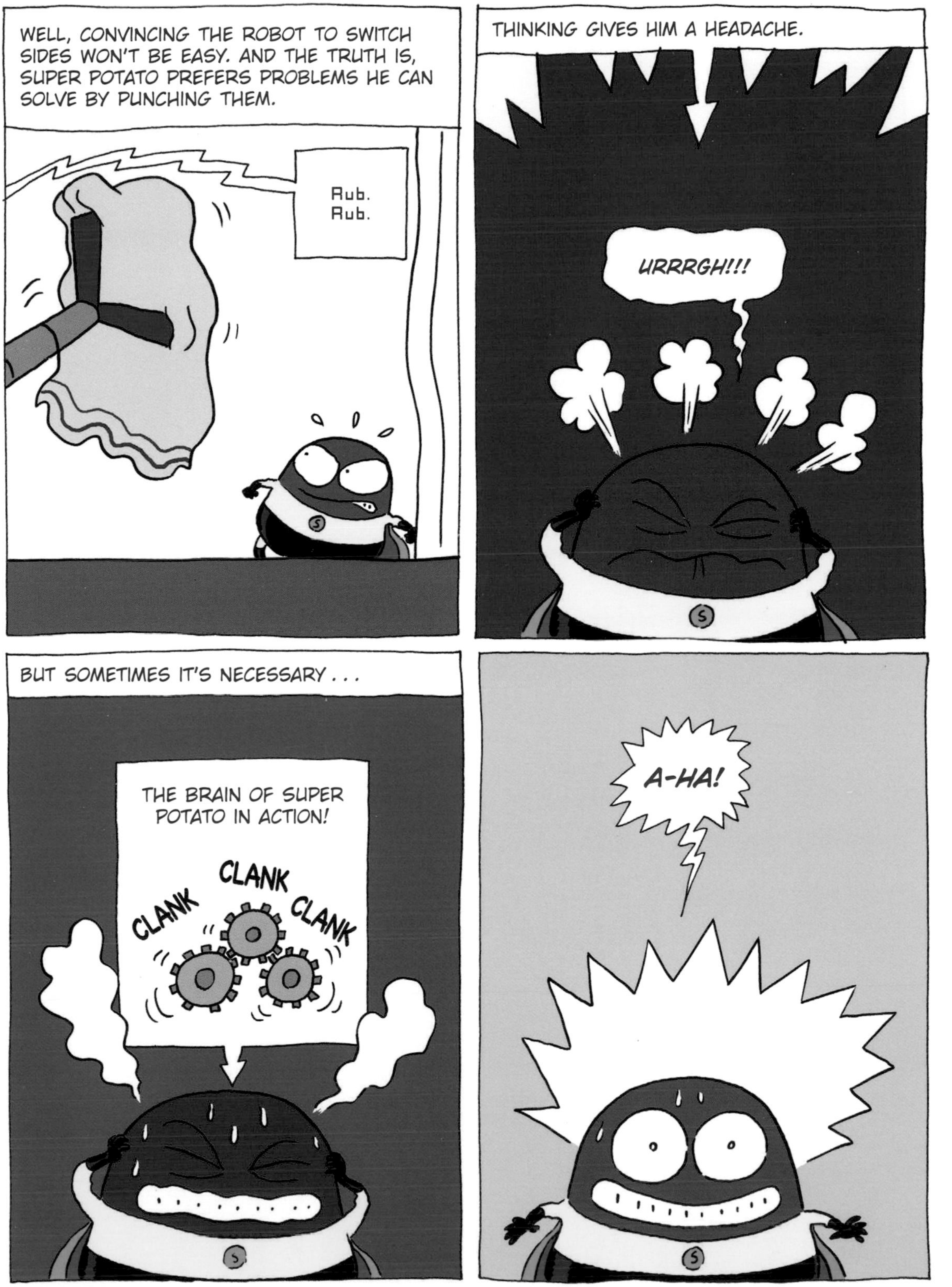
WELL, CONVINCING THE ROBOT TO SWITCH SIDES WON'T BE EASY. AND THE TRUTH IS, SUPER POTATO PREFERS PROBLEMS HE CAN SOLVE BY PUNCHING THEM.
Rub. Rub.
THINKING GIVES HIM A HEADACHE.
URRRGH!!!
BUT SOMETIMES IT'S NECESSARY . . .
THE BRAIN OF SUPER POTATO IN ACTION!
CLANK
CLANK
CLANK
A-HA!

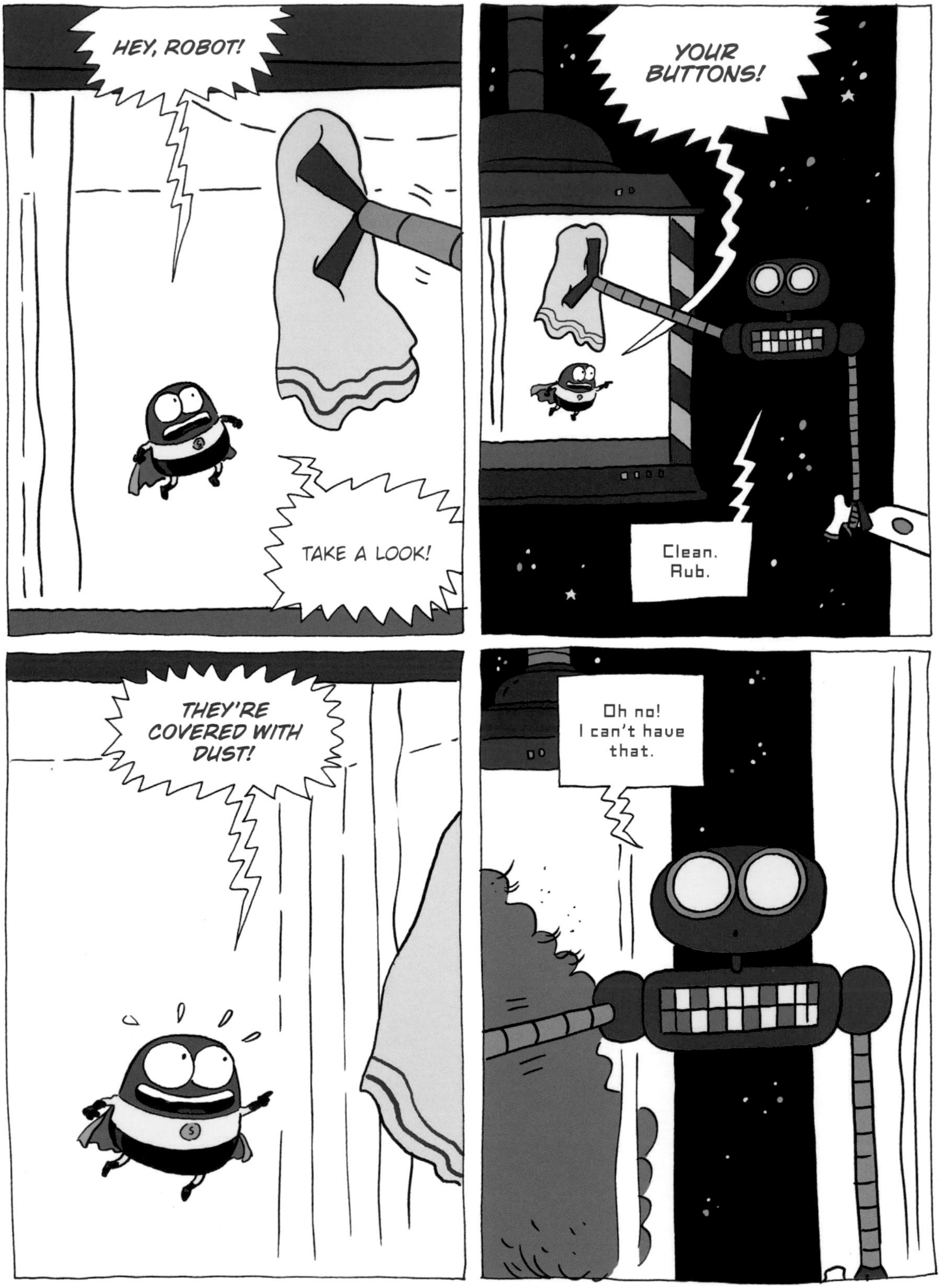
HEY, ROBOT!
TAKE A LOOK!
YOUR BUTTONS!
Clean. Rub.
THEY'RE COVERED WITH DUST!
Oh no! I can't have that.

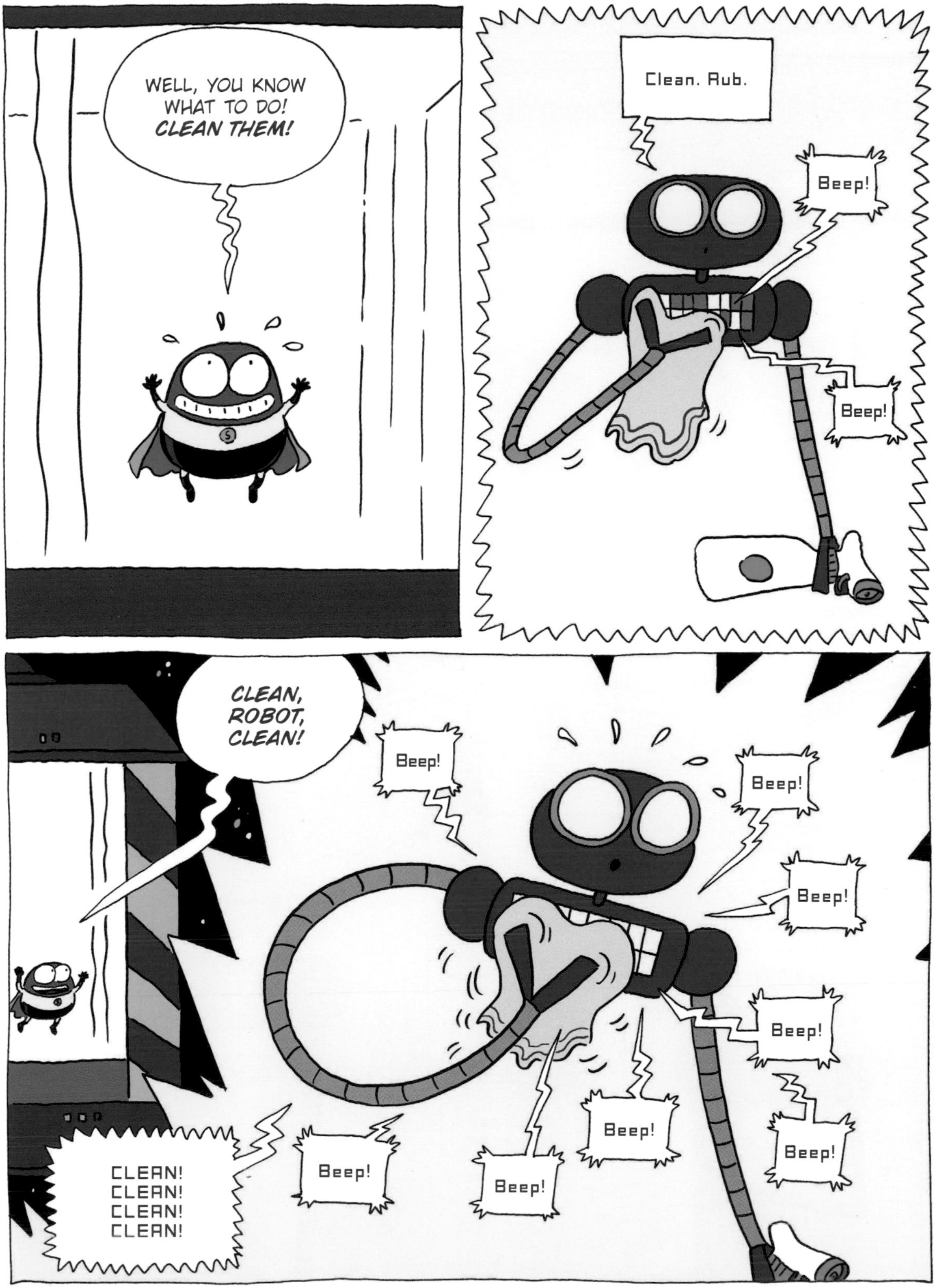
WELL, YOU KNOW WHAT TO DO! CLEAN THEM!
Clean. Rub.
Beep!
Beep!
CLEAN, ROBOT, CLEAN!
Beep!
Beep!
Beep!
Beep!
CLEAN! CLEAN! CLEAN! CLEAN!
Beep!
Beep!
Beep!
Beep!

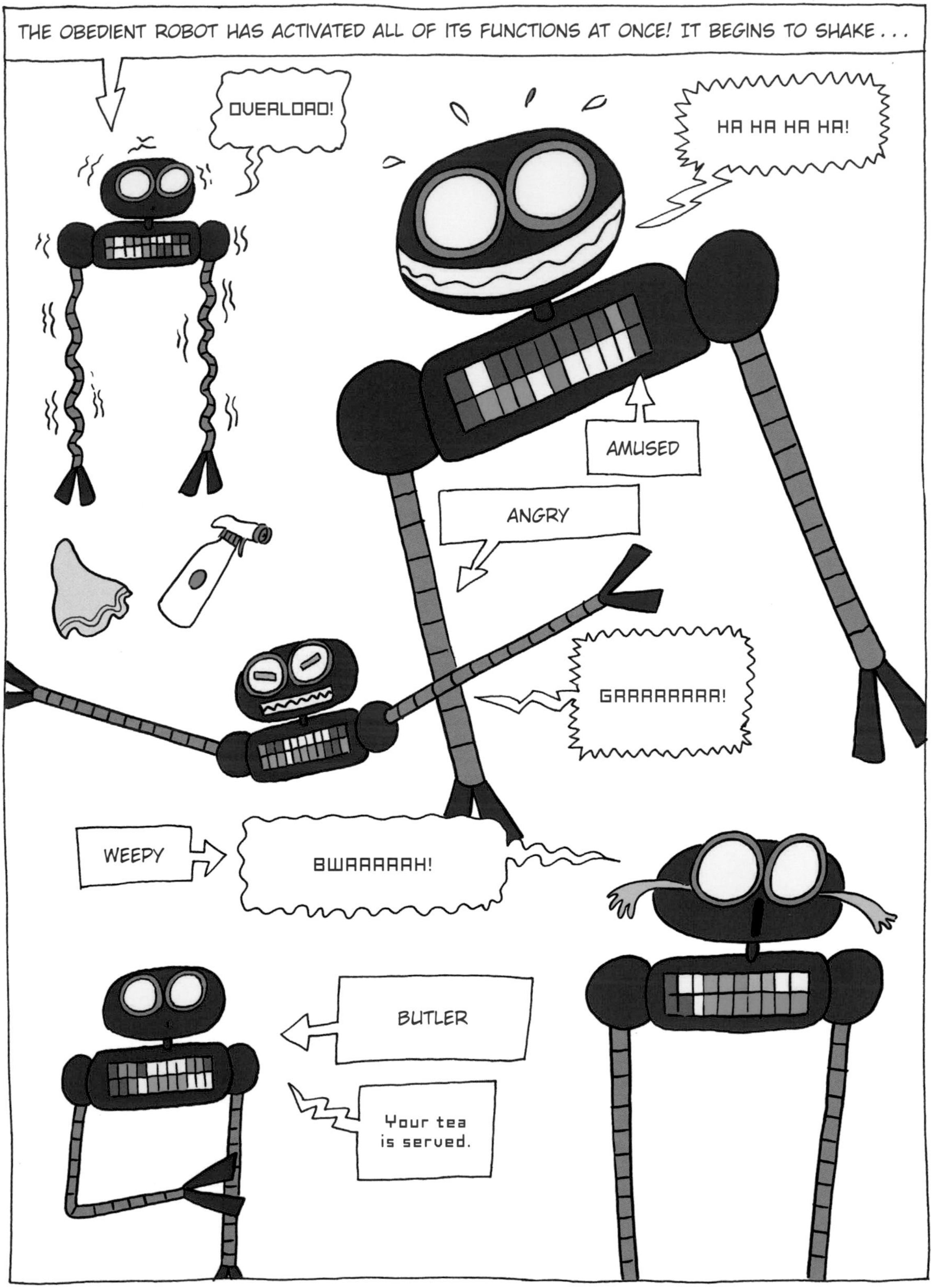
THE OBEDIENT ROBOT HAS ACTIVATED ALL OF ITS FUNCTIONS AT ONCE! IT BEGINS TO SHAKE . . .
OVERLOAD!
HA HA HA HA!
AMUSED
ANGRY
GRRRRRRRR!
WEEPY
BWAAAAAH!
BUTLER
Your tea is served.

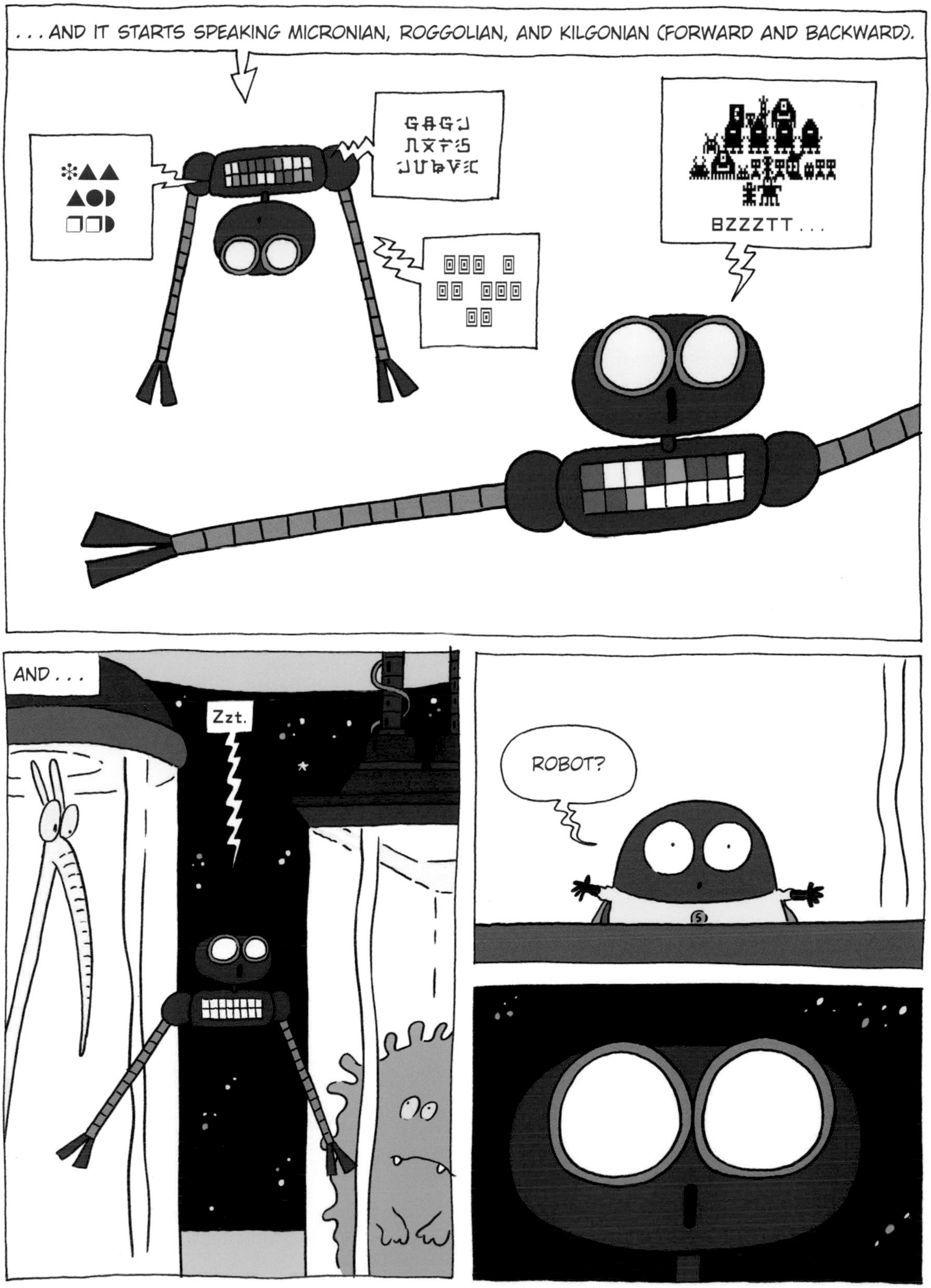

. . . AND IT STARTS SPEAKING MICRONIAN, ROGGOLIAN, AND KILGONIAN (FORWARD AND BACKWARD).
BZZZTT . . .
AND . . .
Zzt.
ROBOT?

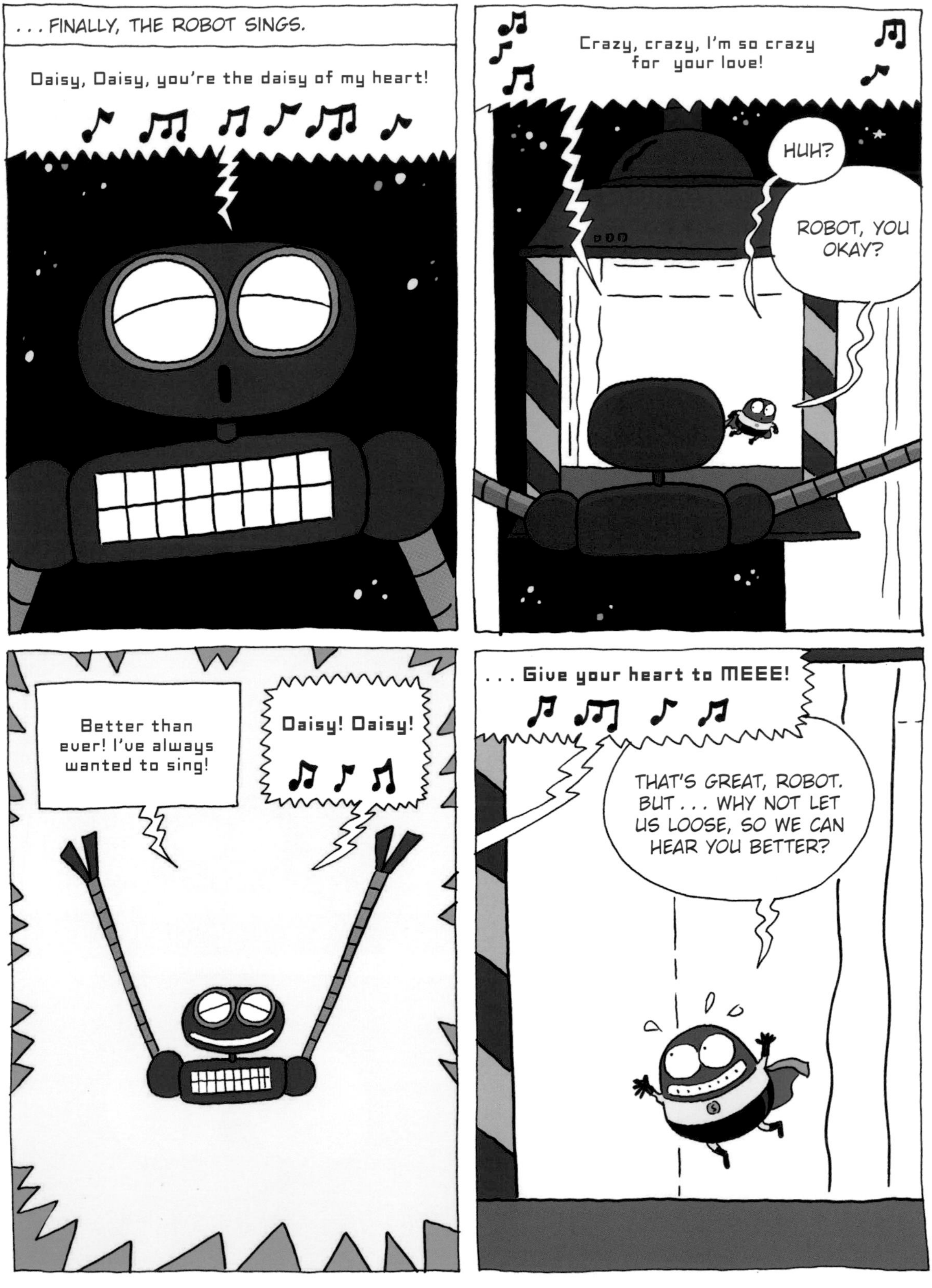
. . . FINALLY, THE ROBOT SINGS.
Daisy, Daisy, you're the daisy of my heart!
Crazy, crazy, I'm so crazy for your love!
HUH?
ROBOT, YOU OKAY?
Better than ever! I've always wanted to sing!
Daisy! Daisy!
. . . Give your heart to MEEE!
THAT'S GREAT, ROBOT. BUT . . . WHY NOT LET US LOOSE, SO WE CAN HEAR YOU BETTER?

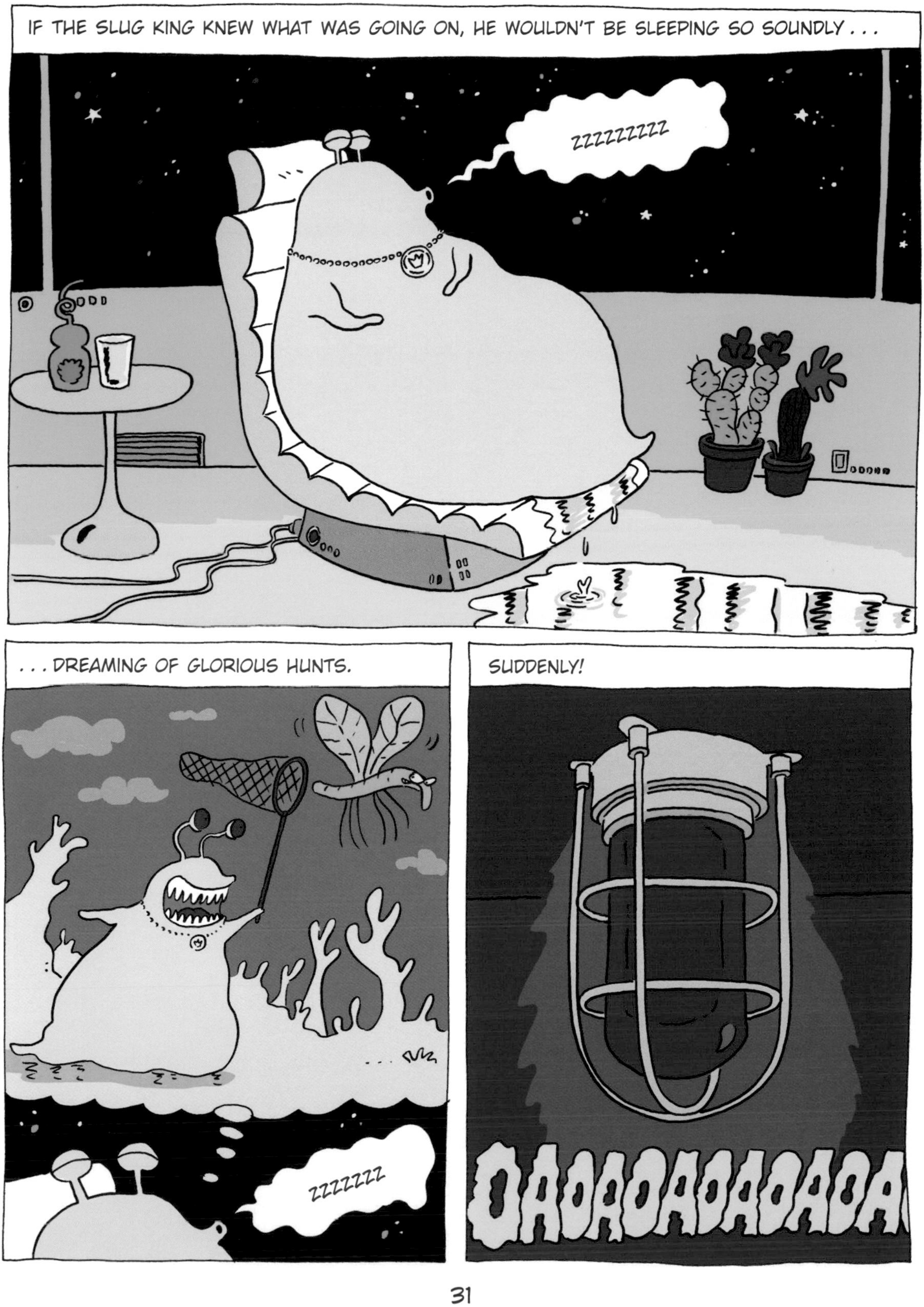
IF THE SLUG KING KNEW WHAT WAS GOING ON, HE WOULDN'T BE SLEEPING SO SOUNDLY . . .
ZZZZZZZZZ
. . . DREAMING OF GLORIOUS HUNTS.
ZZZZZZZ
SUDDENLY!
OAOAOAOAOAOAOA

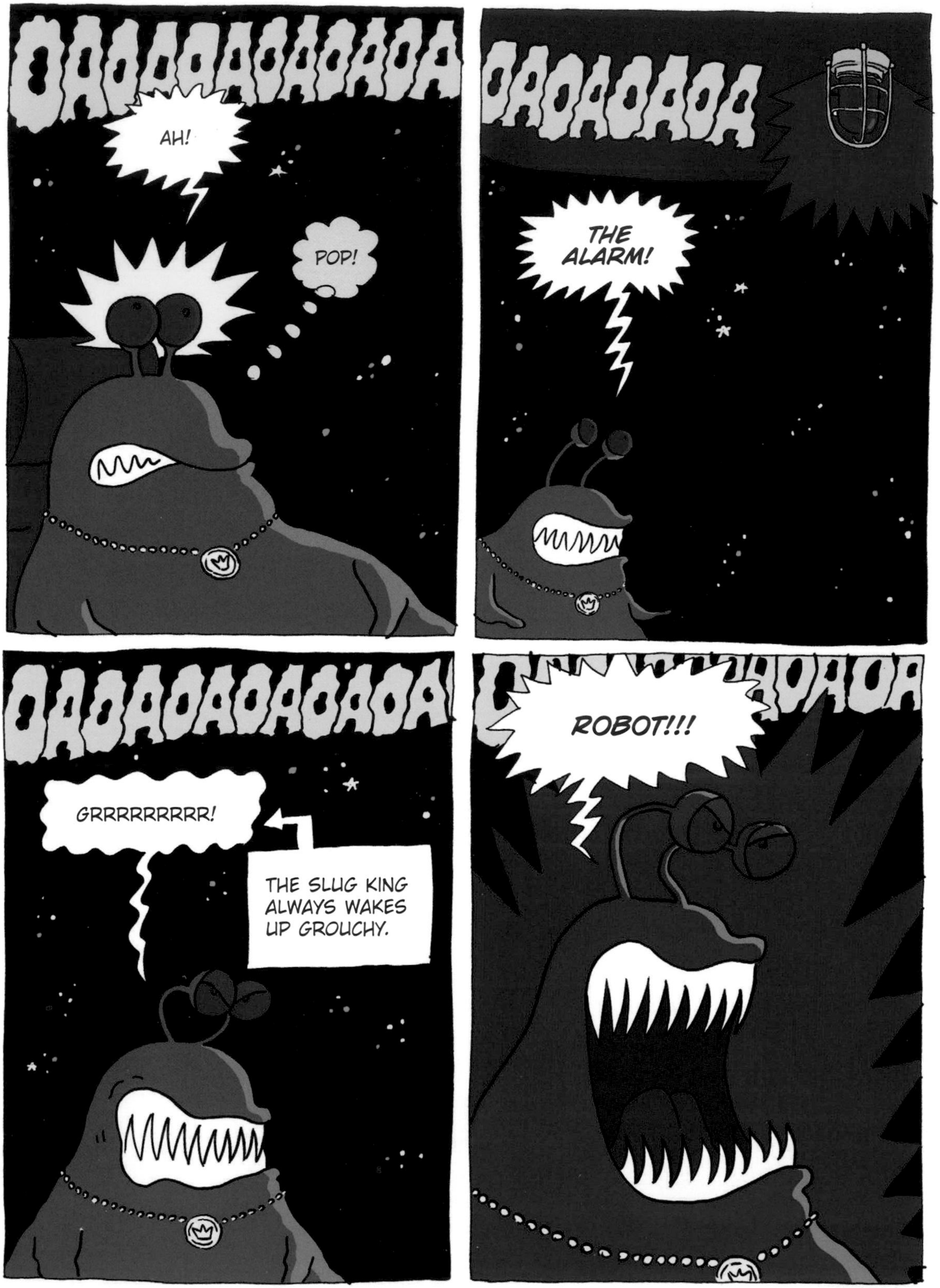
OAOAOAOAOAOA
AH!
POP!
OAOAOAOAOA
THE ALARM!
OAOAOAOAOAOAOA
GRRRRRRRRR!
THE SLUG KING ALWAYS WAKES UP GROUCHY.
ROBOT!!!

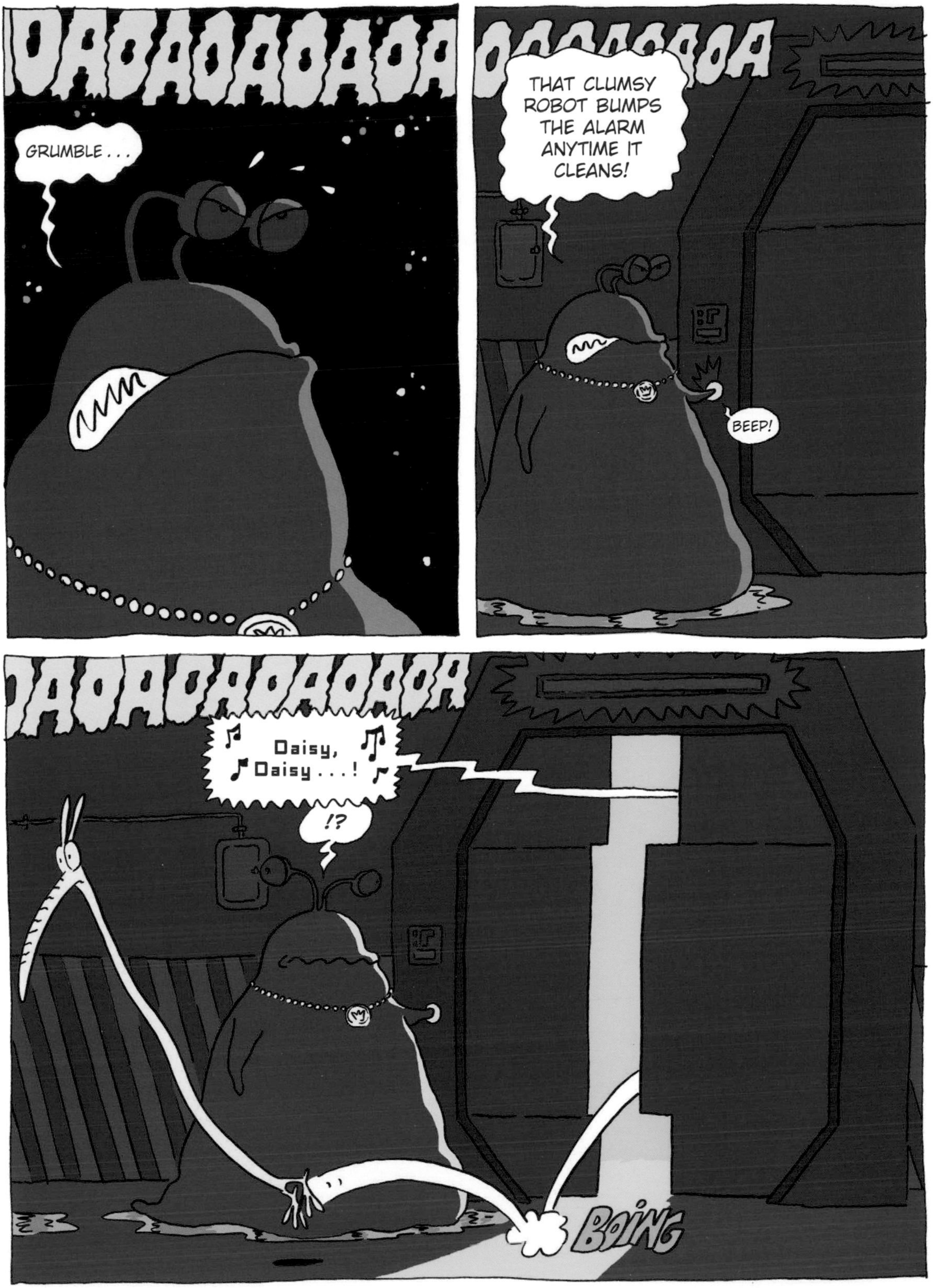
GRUMBLE . . .
THAT CLUMSY ROBOT BUMPS THE ALARM ANYTIME IT CLEANS!
BEEP!
Daisy, Daisy . . . !
!?
BOING

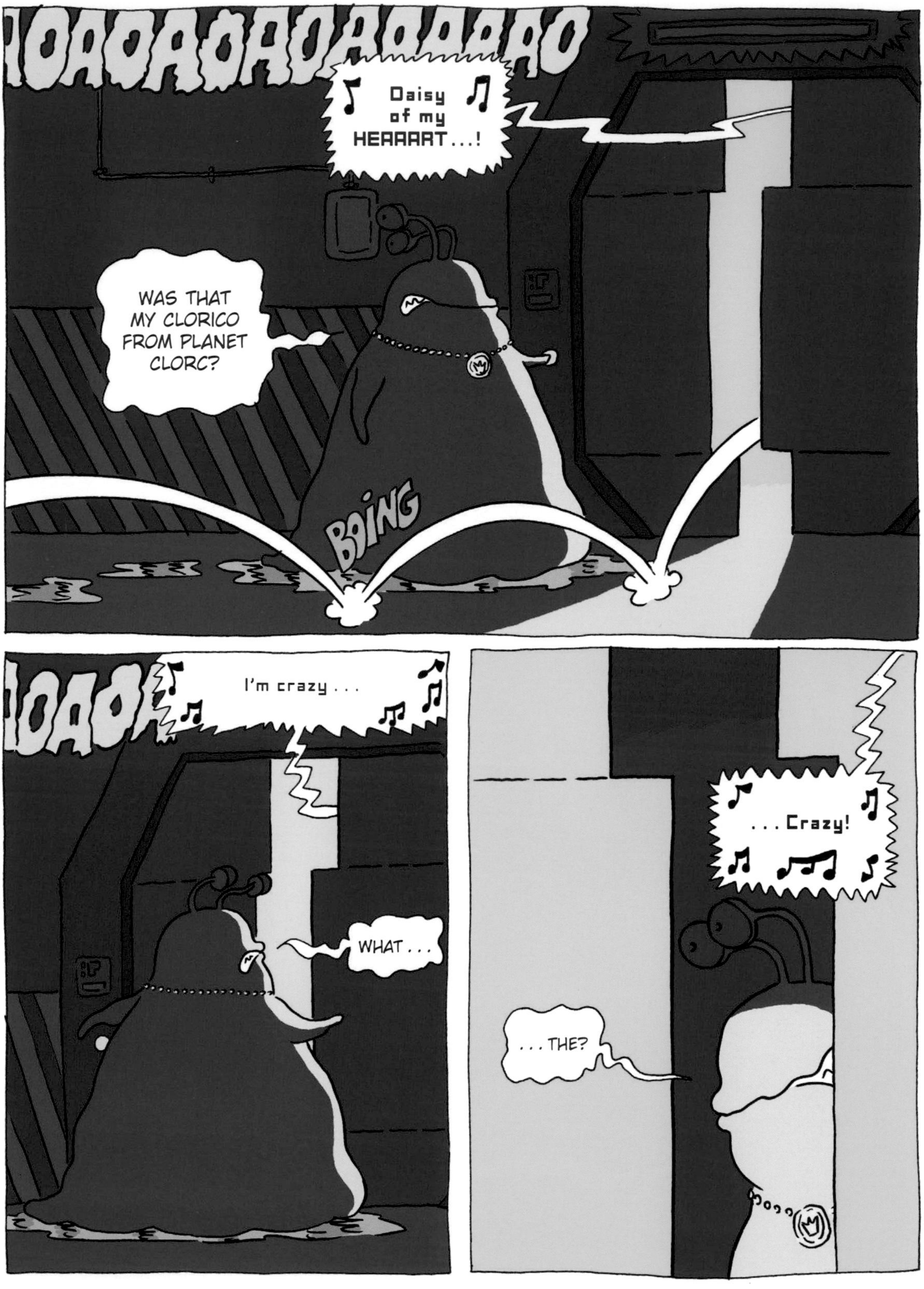
AOAOAOAOAOAOAOAOAO
Daisy of my HEARRRT...!
WAS THAT MY CLORICO FROM PLANET CLORC?
BOING
AOAOA
I'm crazy . . .
WHAT . . .
. . . Crazy!
. . . THE?

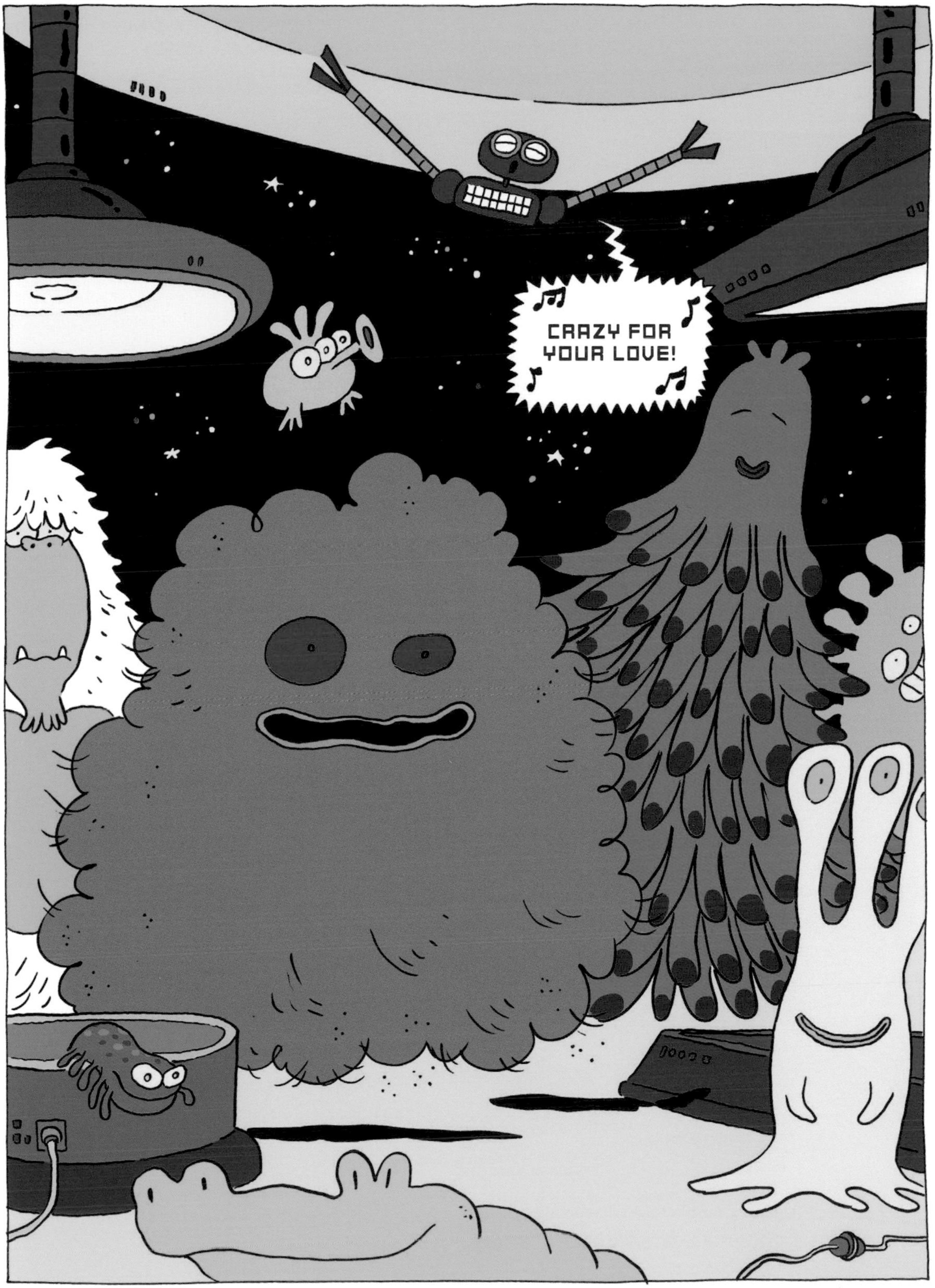
CRAZY FOR YOUR LOVE!

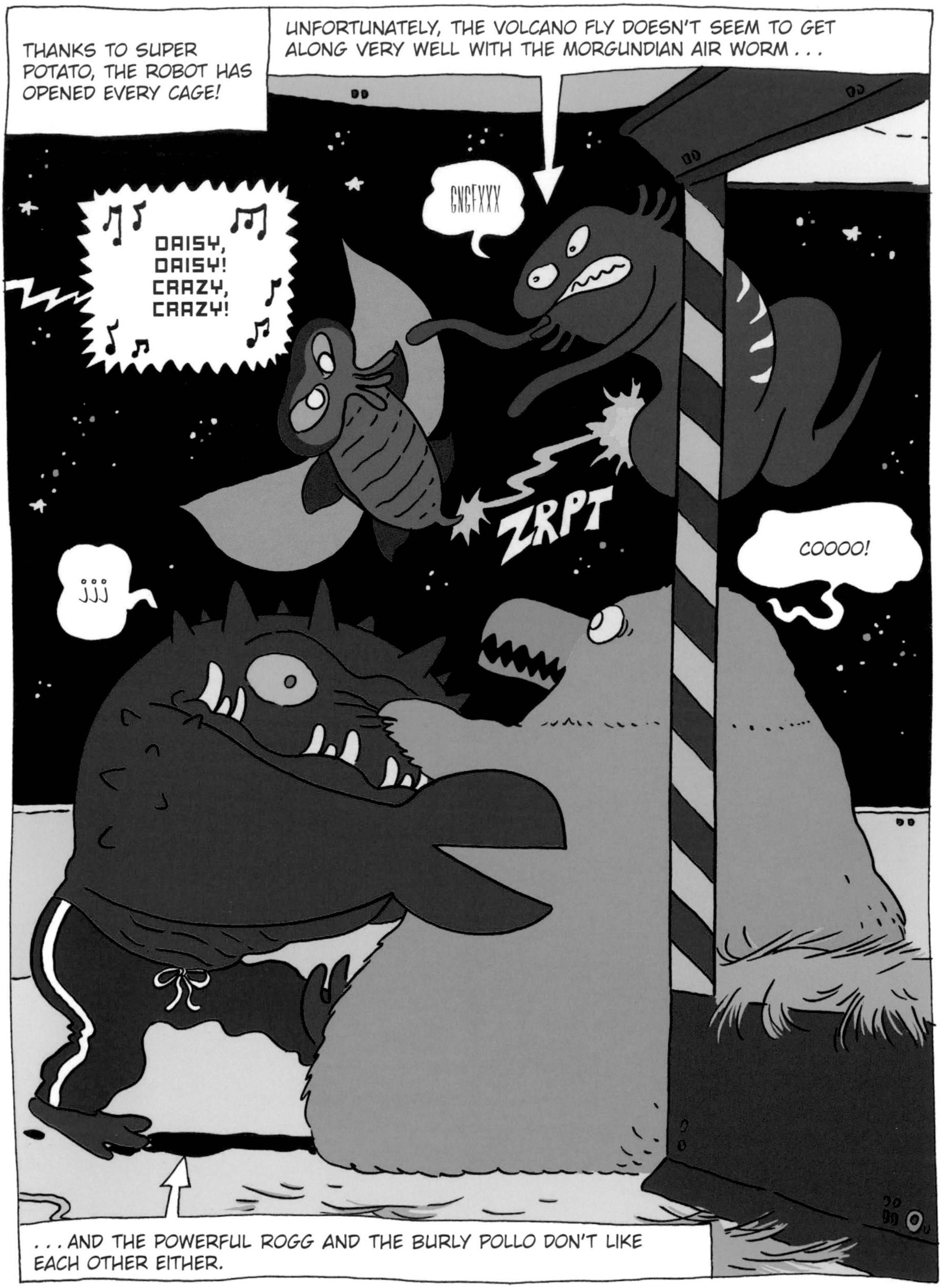
THANKS TO SUPER POTATO, THE ROBOT HAS OPENED EVERY CAGE!
UNFORTUNATELY, THE VOLCANO FLY DOESN'T SEEM TO GET ALONG VERY WELL WITH THE MORGUNDIAN AIR WORM . . .
DAISY, DAISY! CRAZY, CRAZY!
GNGFXXX
ZRPT
COOOO!
. . . AND THE POWERFUL ROGG AND THE BURLY POLLO DON'T LIKE EACH OTHER EITHER.

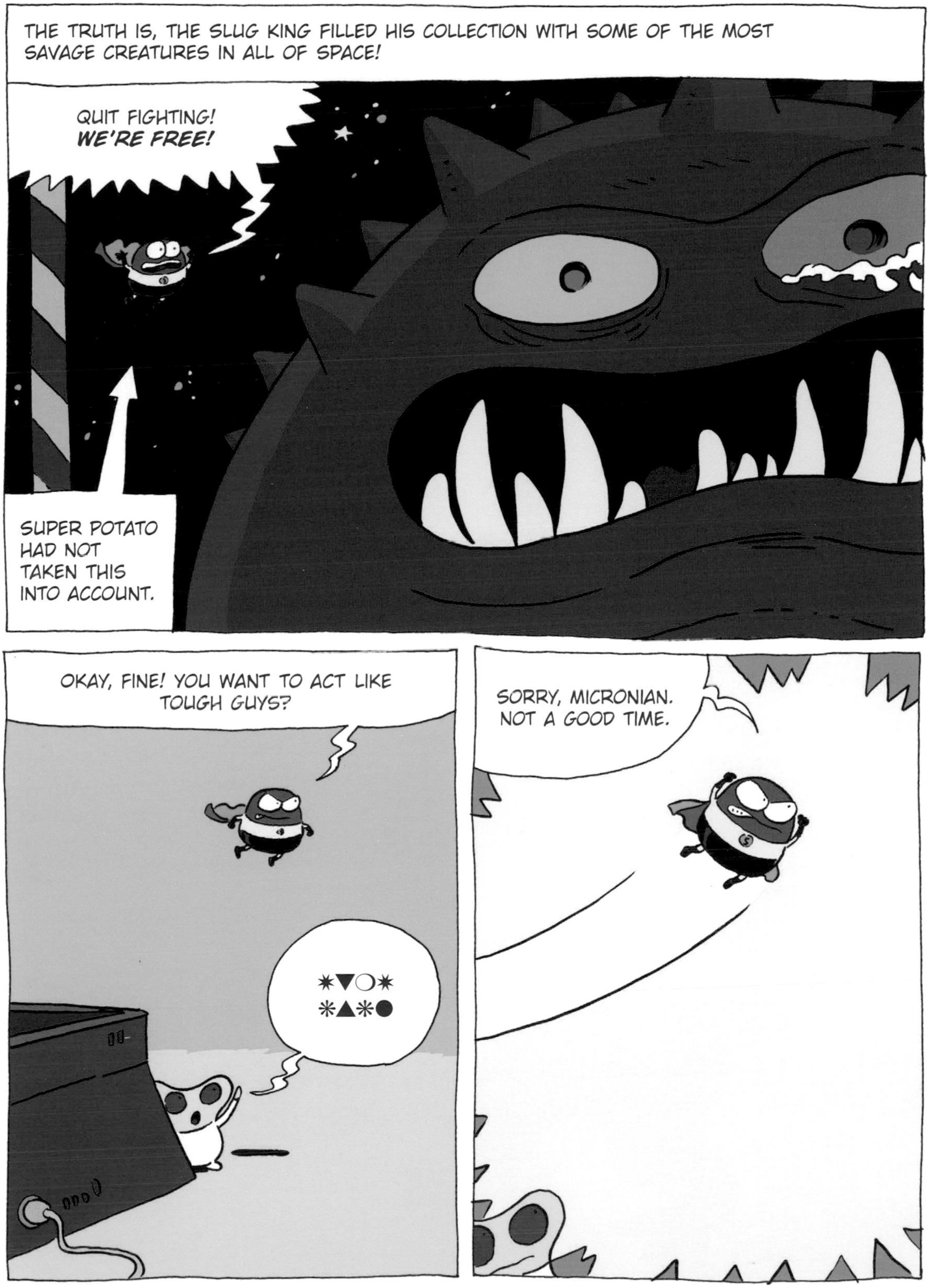
THE TRUTH IS, THE SLUG KING FILLED HIS COLLECTION WITH SOME OF THE MOST SAVAGE CREATURES IN ALL OF SPACE!
QUIT FIGHTING! **WE'RE FREE!**
SUPER POTATO HAD NOT TAKEN THIS INTO ACCOUNT.
OKAY, FINE! YOU WANT TO ACT LIKE TOUGH GUYS?
✶▼○✶ ✳▲✳●
SORRY, MICRONIAN. NOT A GOOD TIME.

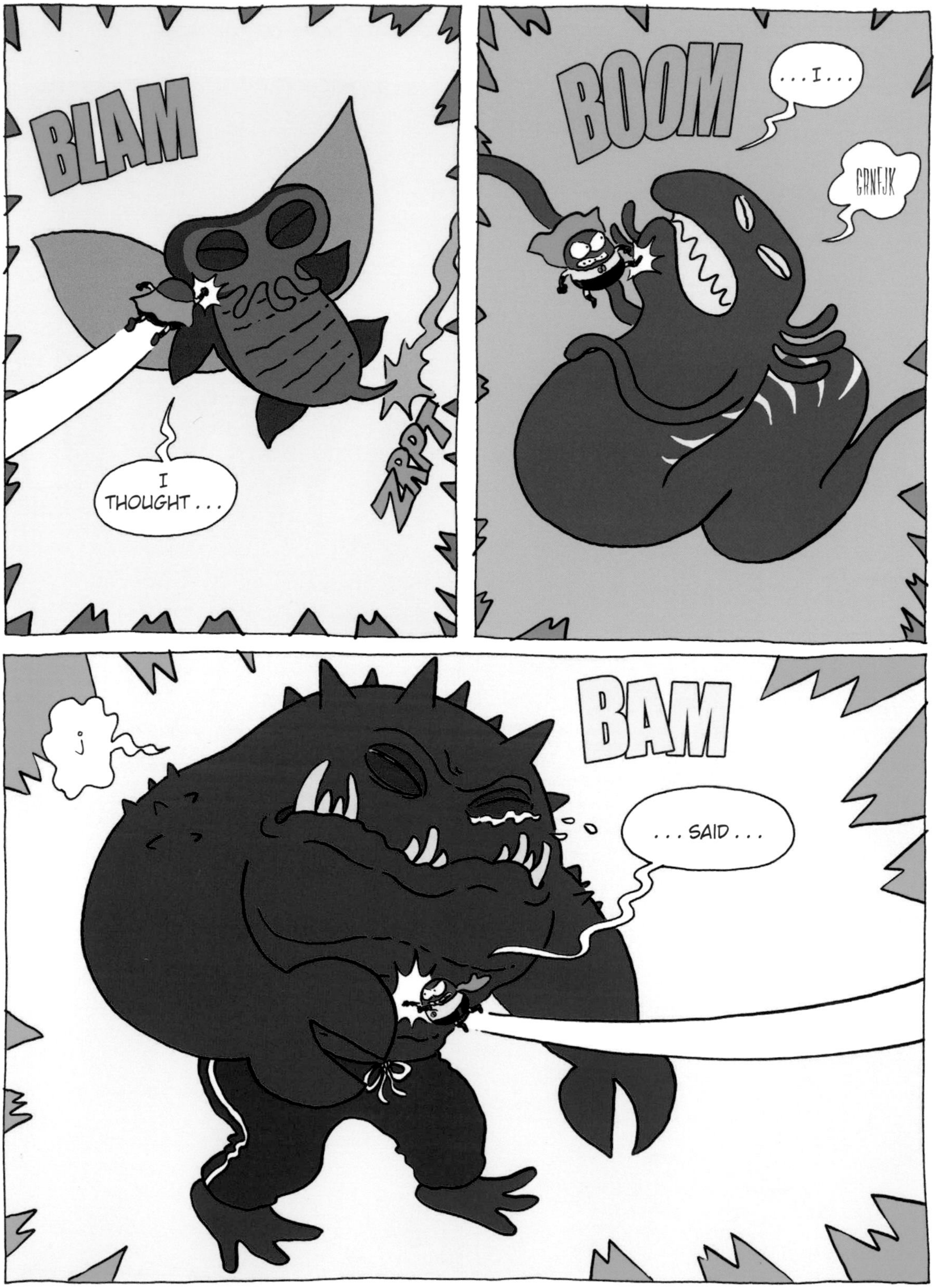
BLAM
I THOUGHT . . .
ZRPT
BOOM
. . . I . . .
GRNFJK
j
BAM
. . . SAID . . .

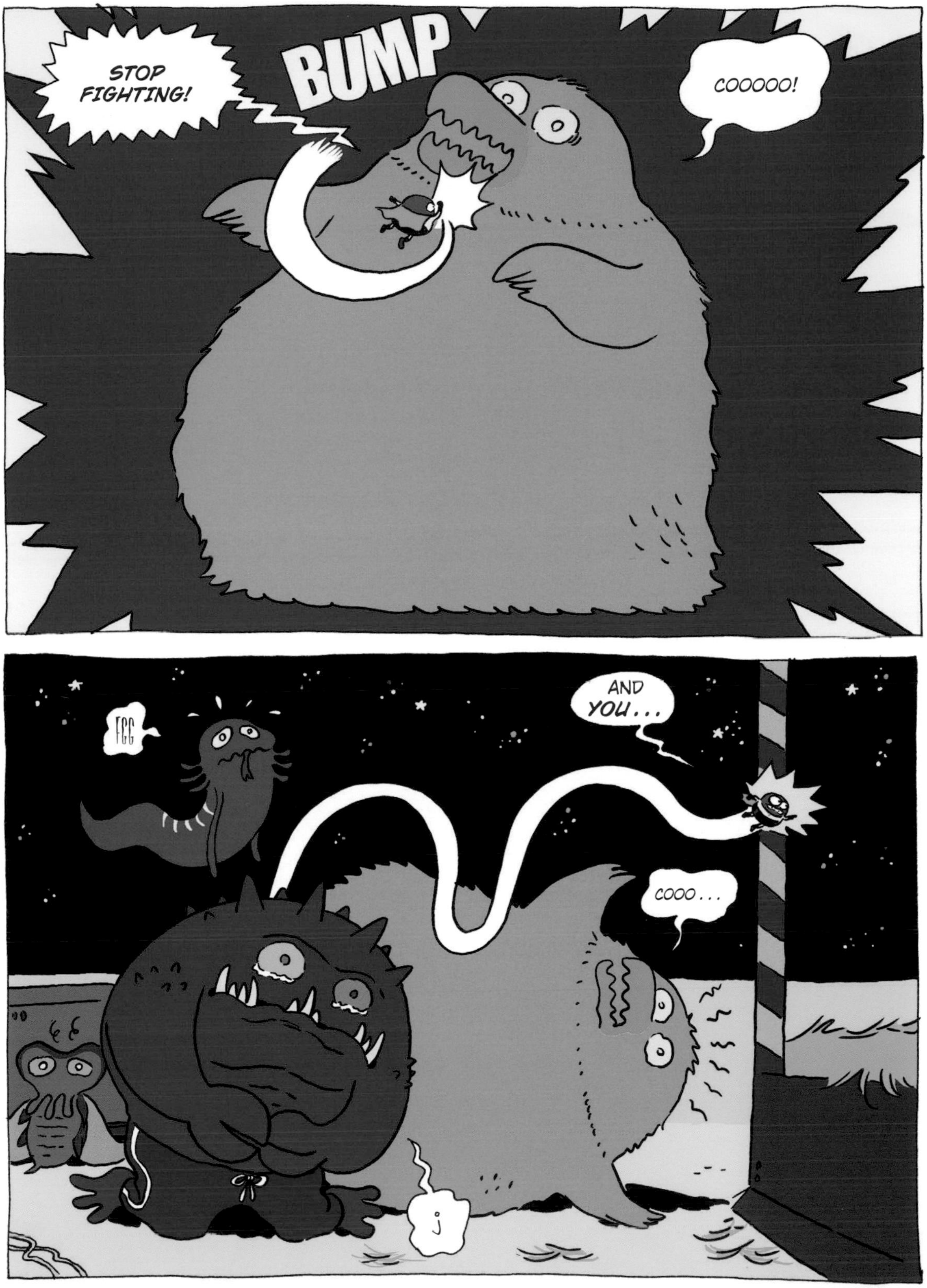
STOP FIGHTING!
BUMP
COOOOO!
AND YOU...
COOO...

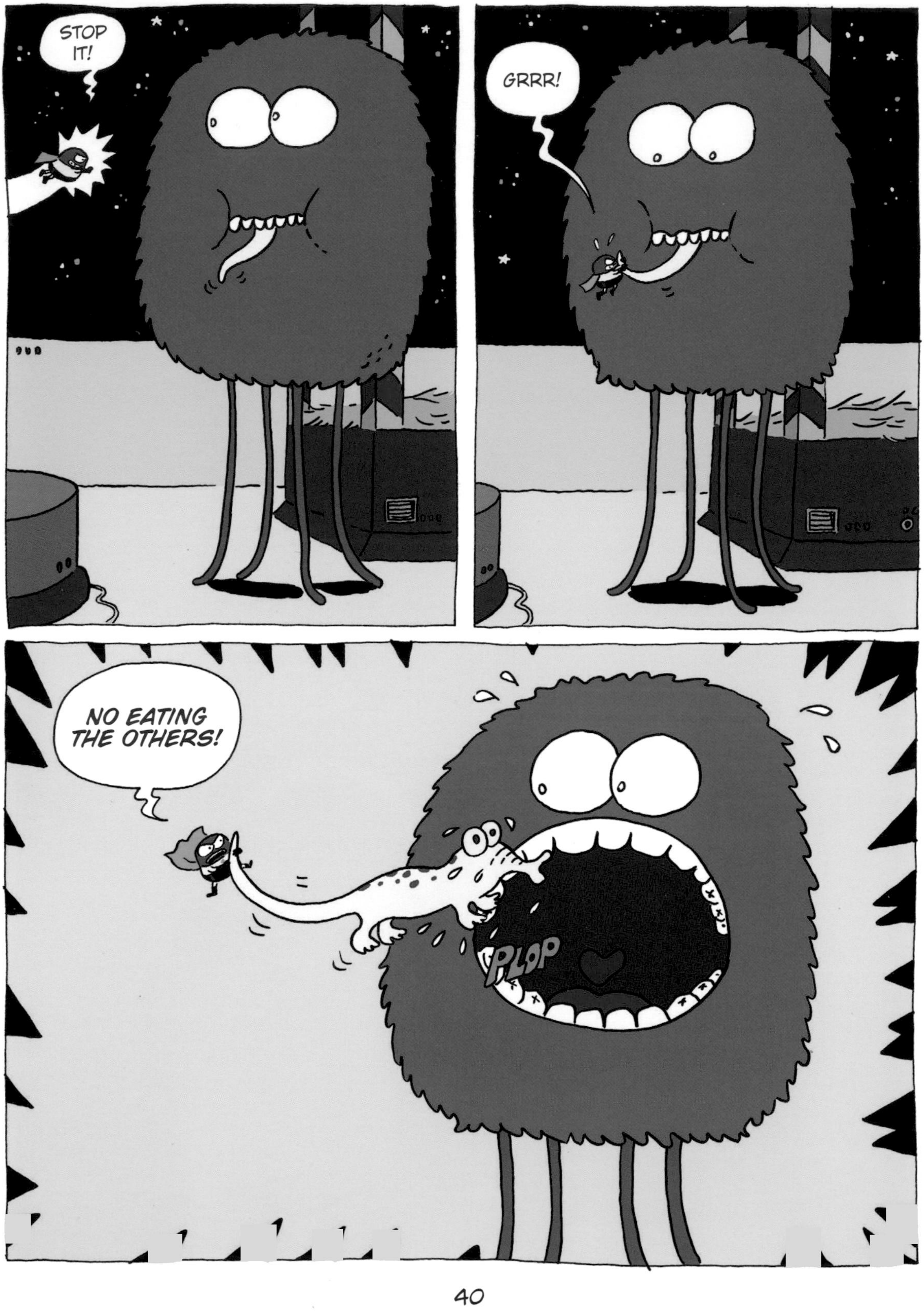
STOP IT!
GRRR!
NO EATING THE OTHERS!
PLOP

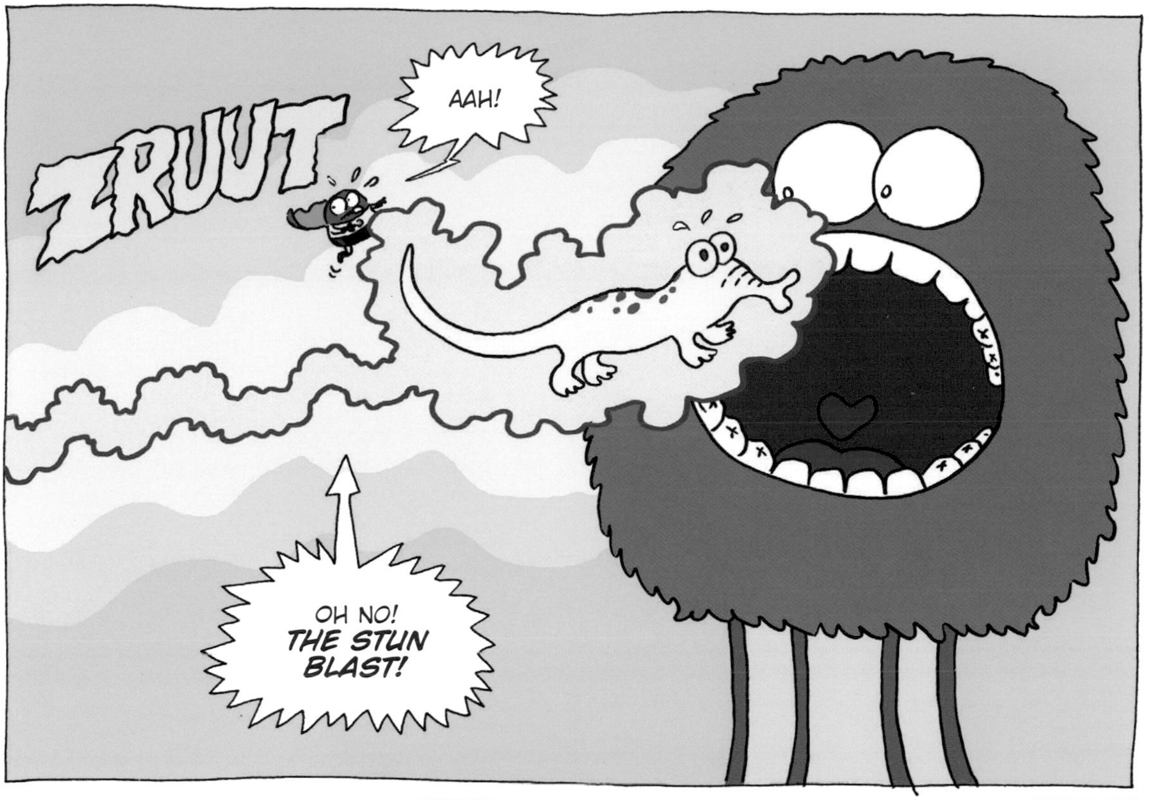
ZRUUT
AAH!
OH NO! THE STUN BLAST!

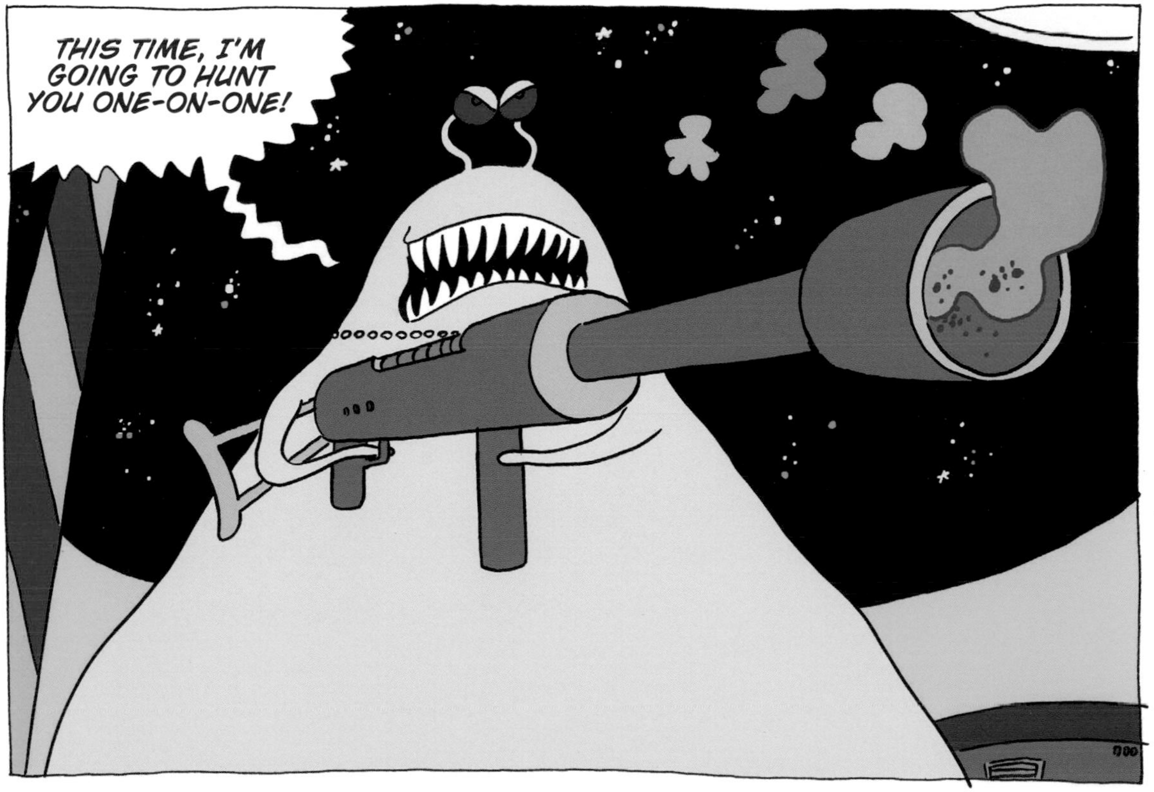
THIS TIME, I'M GOING TO HUNT YOU ONE-ON-ONE!

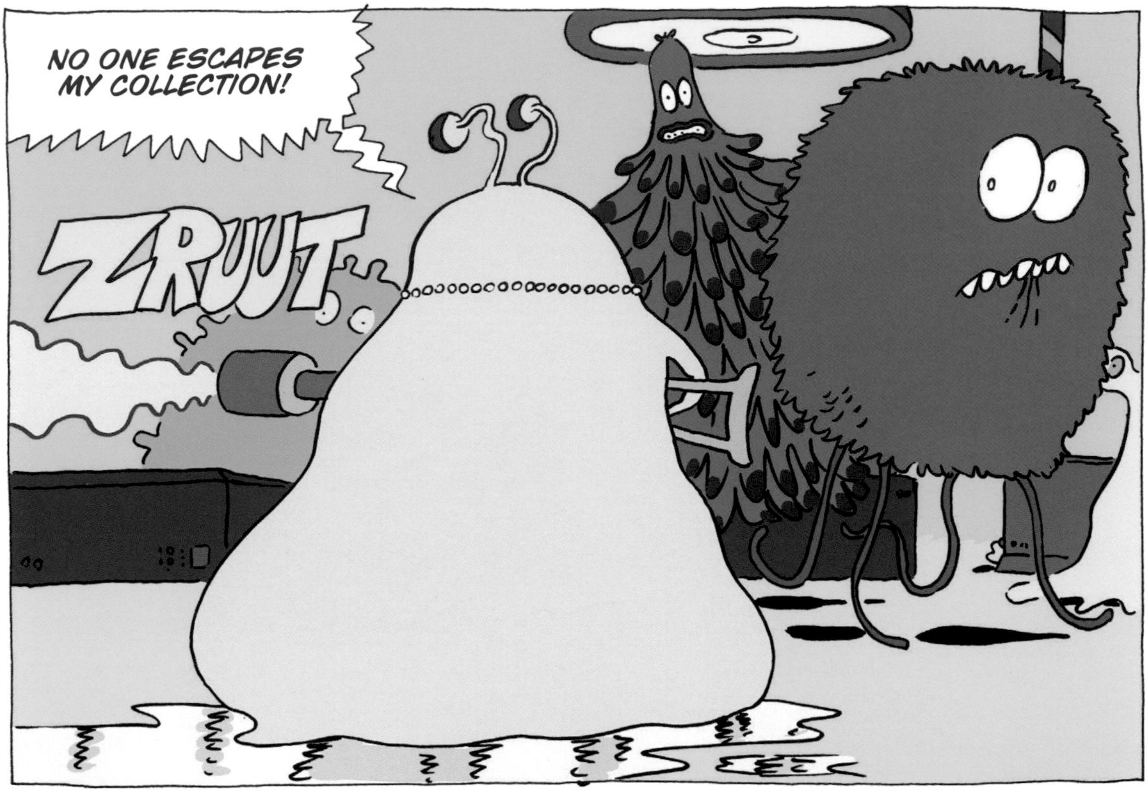
NO ONE ESCAPES MY COLLECTION!
ZRUUT

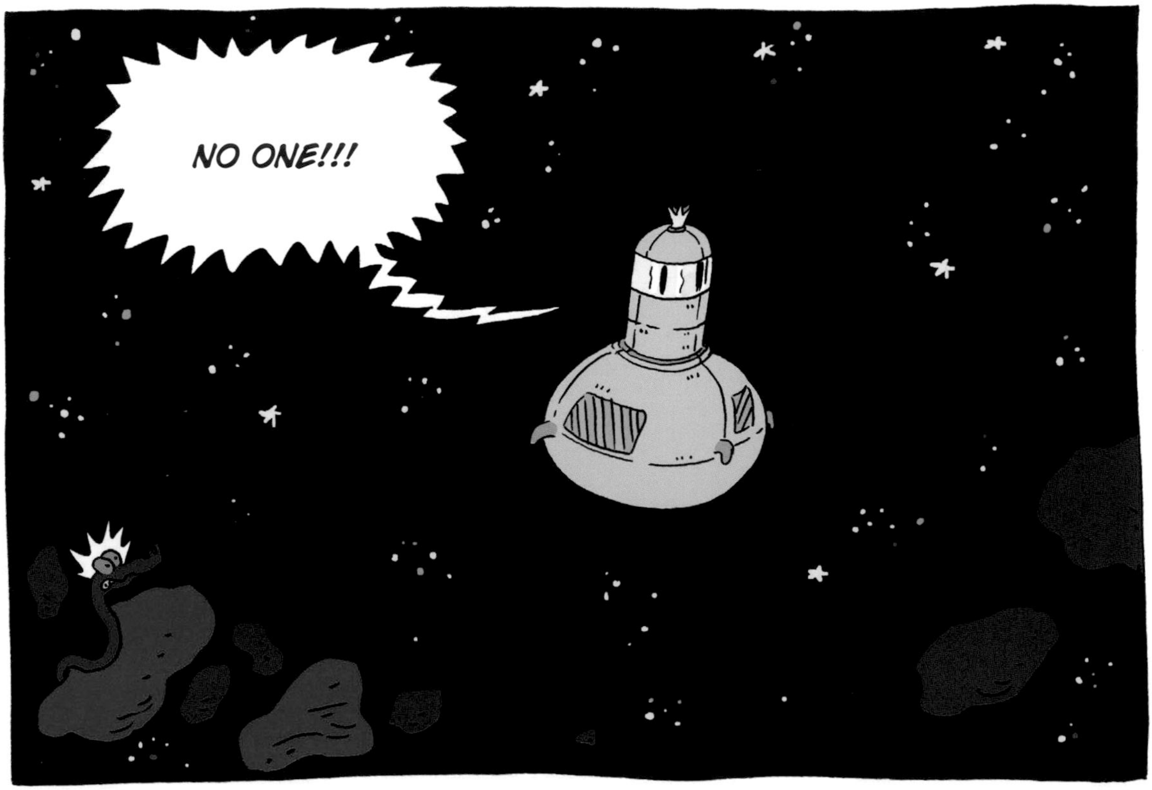
NO ONE!!!

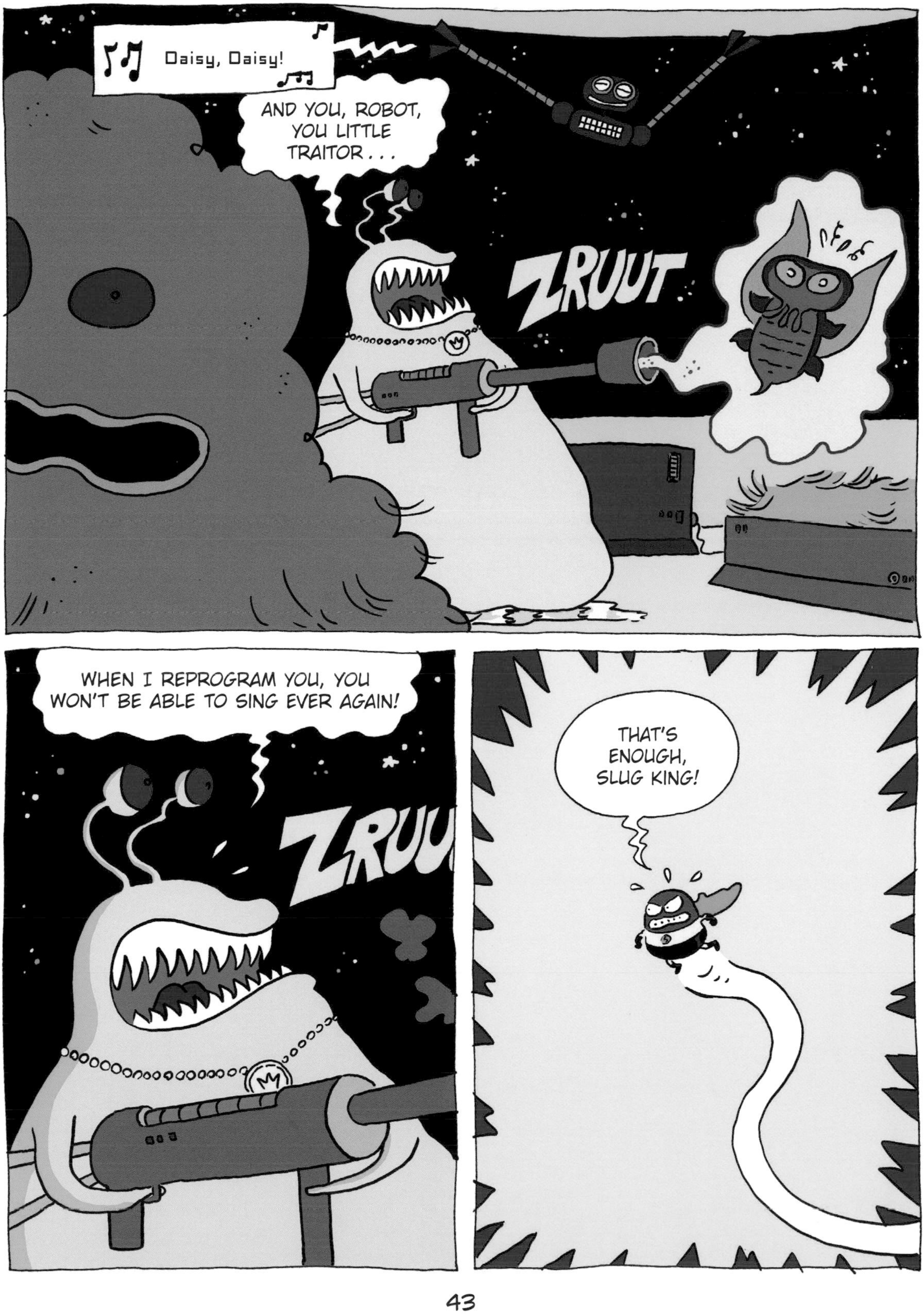
Daisy, Daisy!
AND YOU, ROBOT, YOU LITTLE TRAITOR . . .
ZRUUT
WHEN I REPROGRAM YOU, YOU WON'T BE ABLE TO SING EVER AGAIN!
THAT'S ENOUGH, SLUG KING!

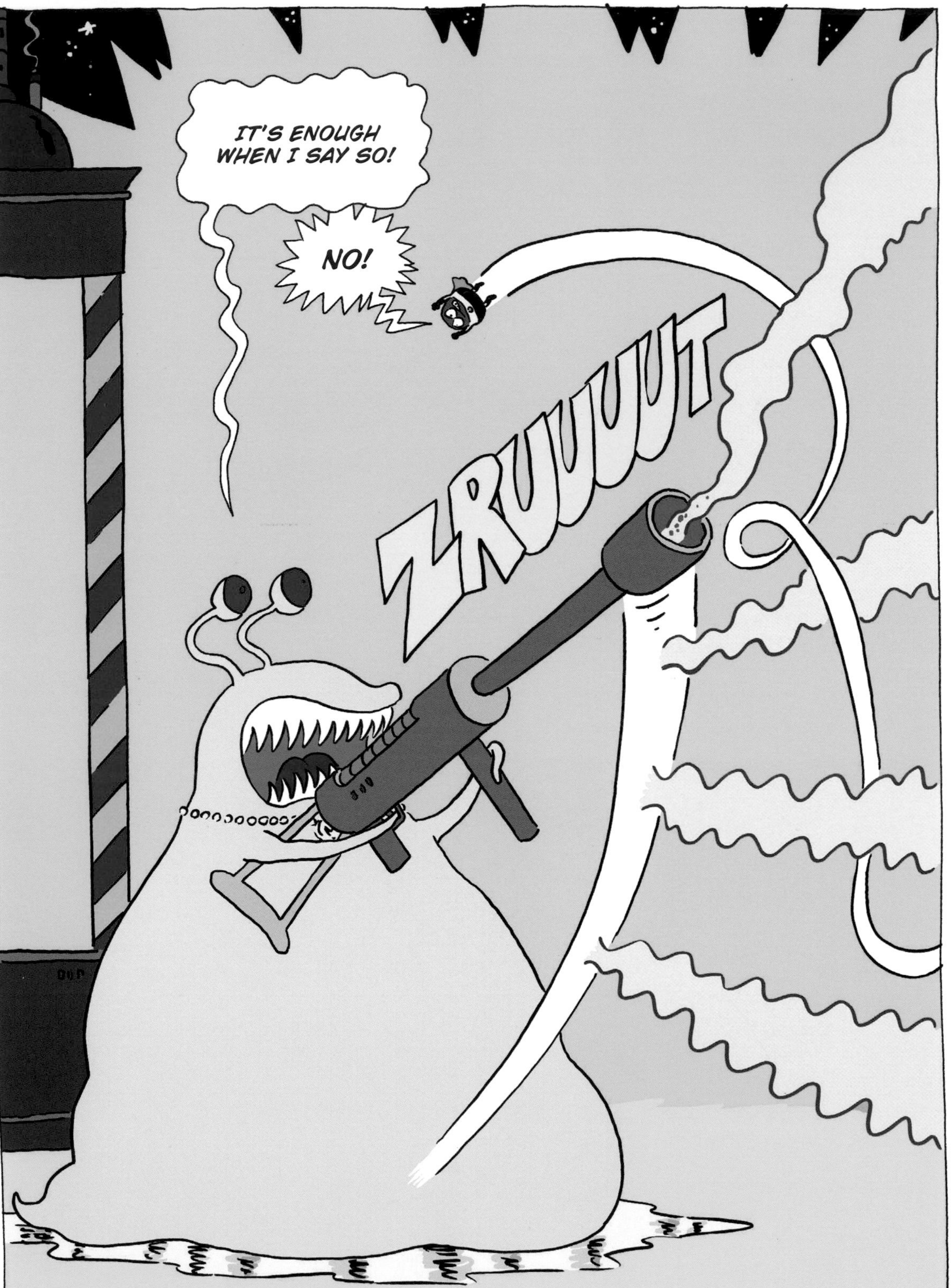
IT'S ENOUGH WHEN I SAY SO!
NO!
ZRUUUUT

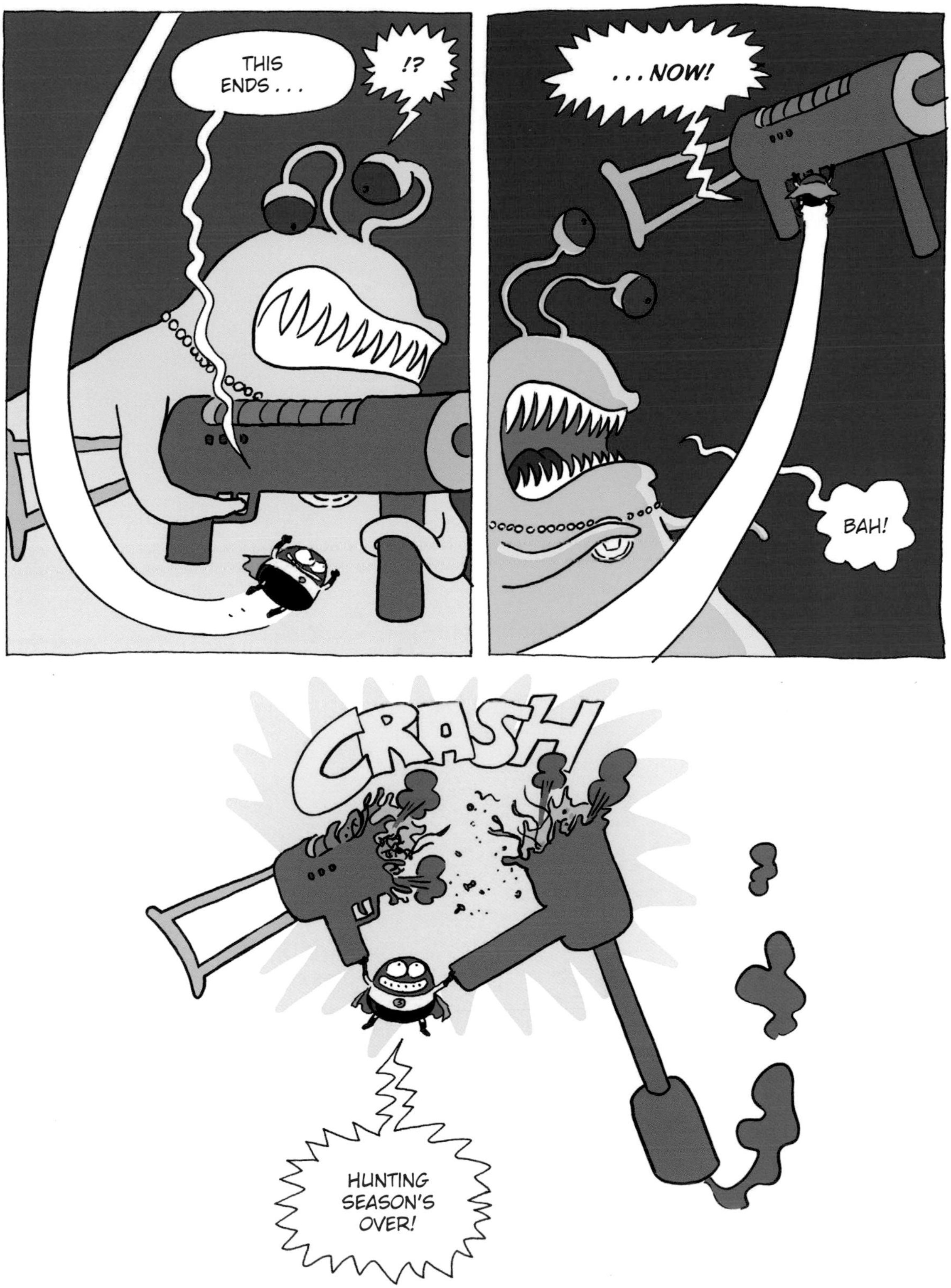
THIS ENDS . . .
!?
. . . NOW!
BAH!
CRASH
HUNTING SEASON'S OVER!

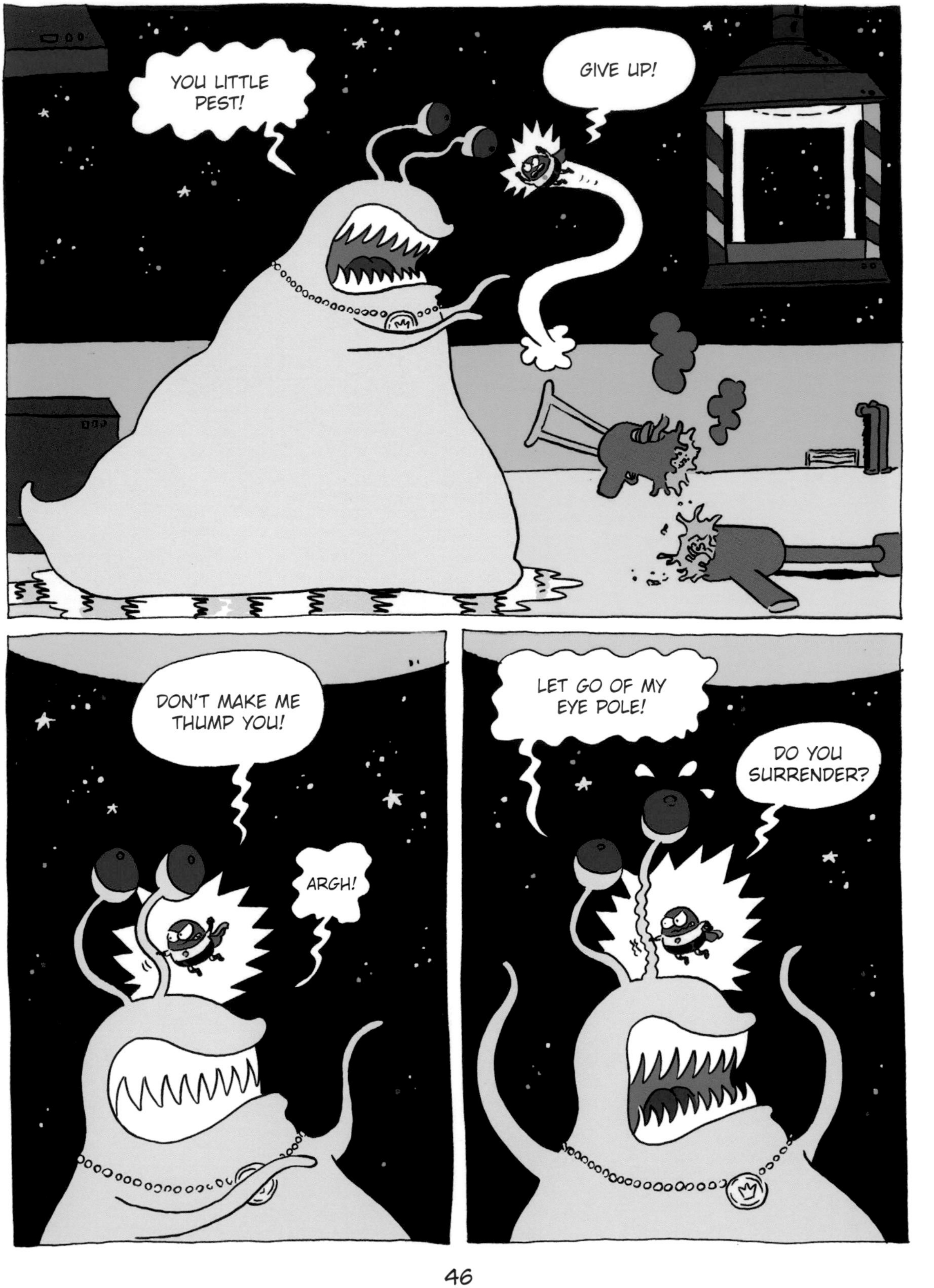
YOU LITTLE PEST!
GIVE UP!
DON'T MAKE ME THUMP YOU!
ARGH!
LET GO OF MY EYE POLE!
DO YOU SURRENDER?

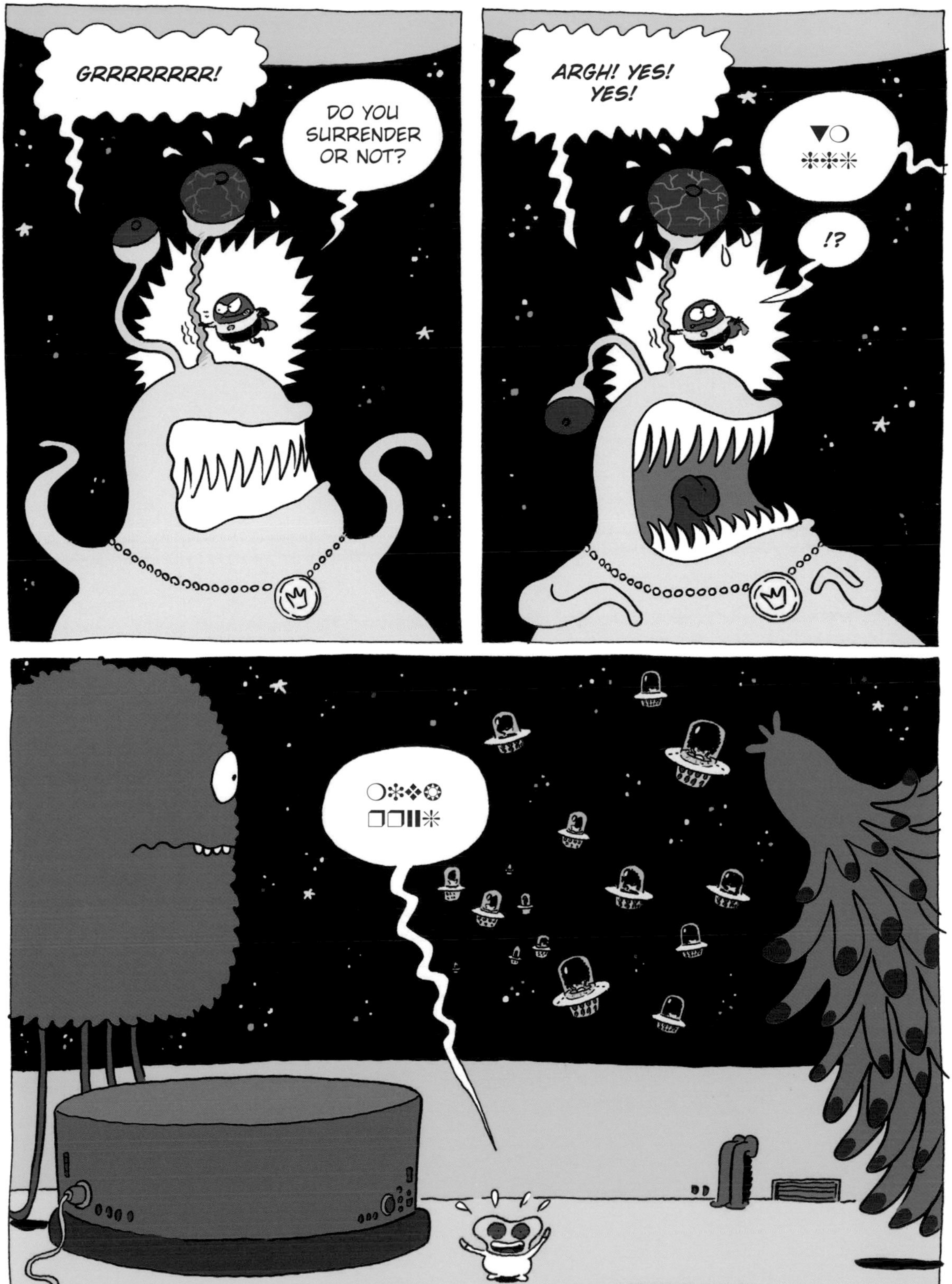
GRRRRRRRR!
DO YOU SURRENDER OR NOT?
ARGH! YES! YES!
!?

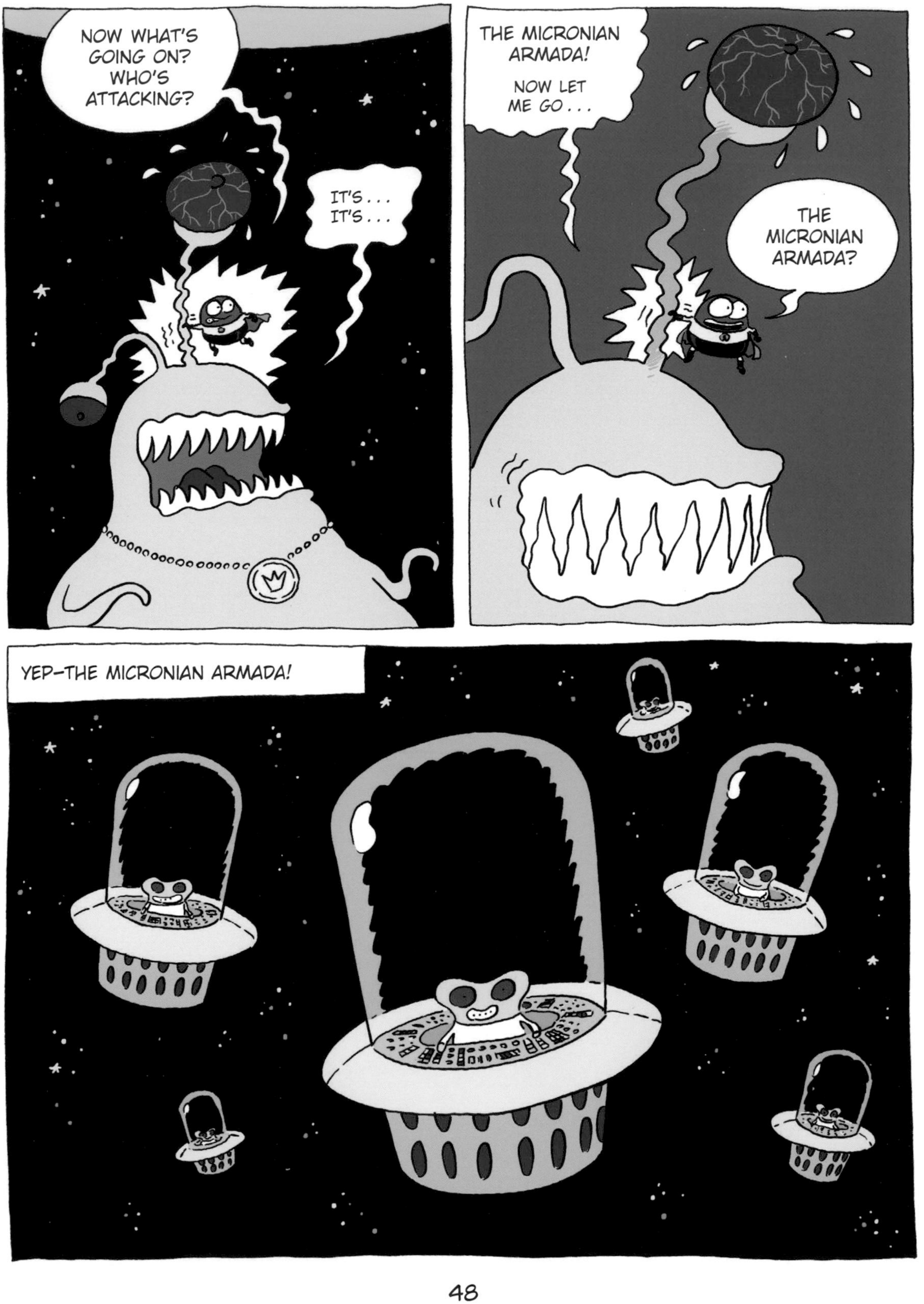
NOW WHAT'S GOING ON? WHO'S ATTACKING?
IT'S . . . IT'S . . .
THE MICRONIAN ARMADA!
NOW LET ME GO . . .
THE MICRONIAN ARMADA?
YEP–THE MICRONIAN ARMADA!

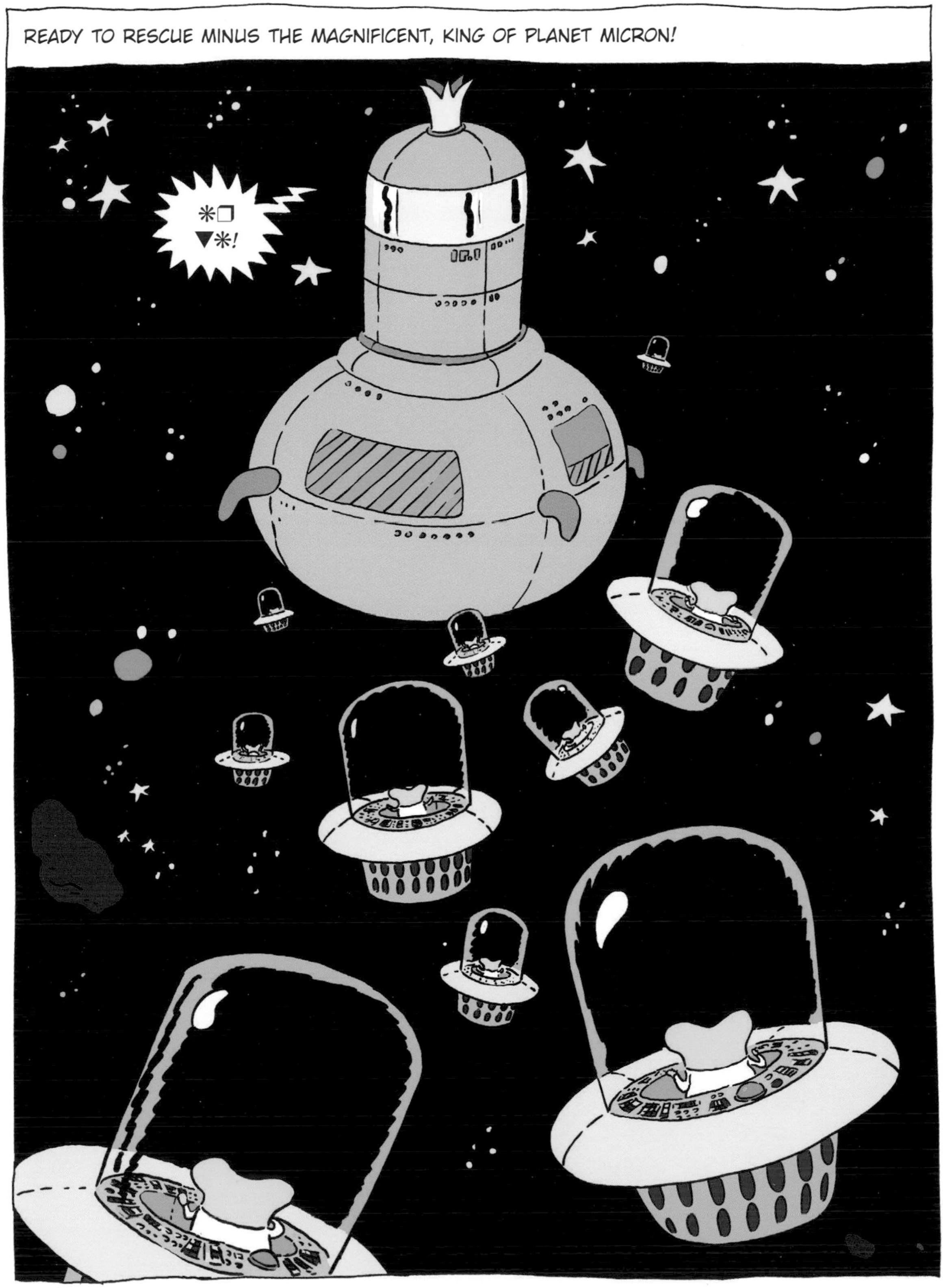
READY TO RESCUE MINUS THE MAGNIFICENT, KING OF PLANET MICRON!
✻❒ ▼✻!

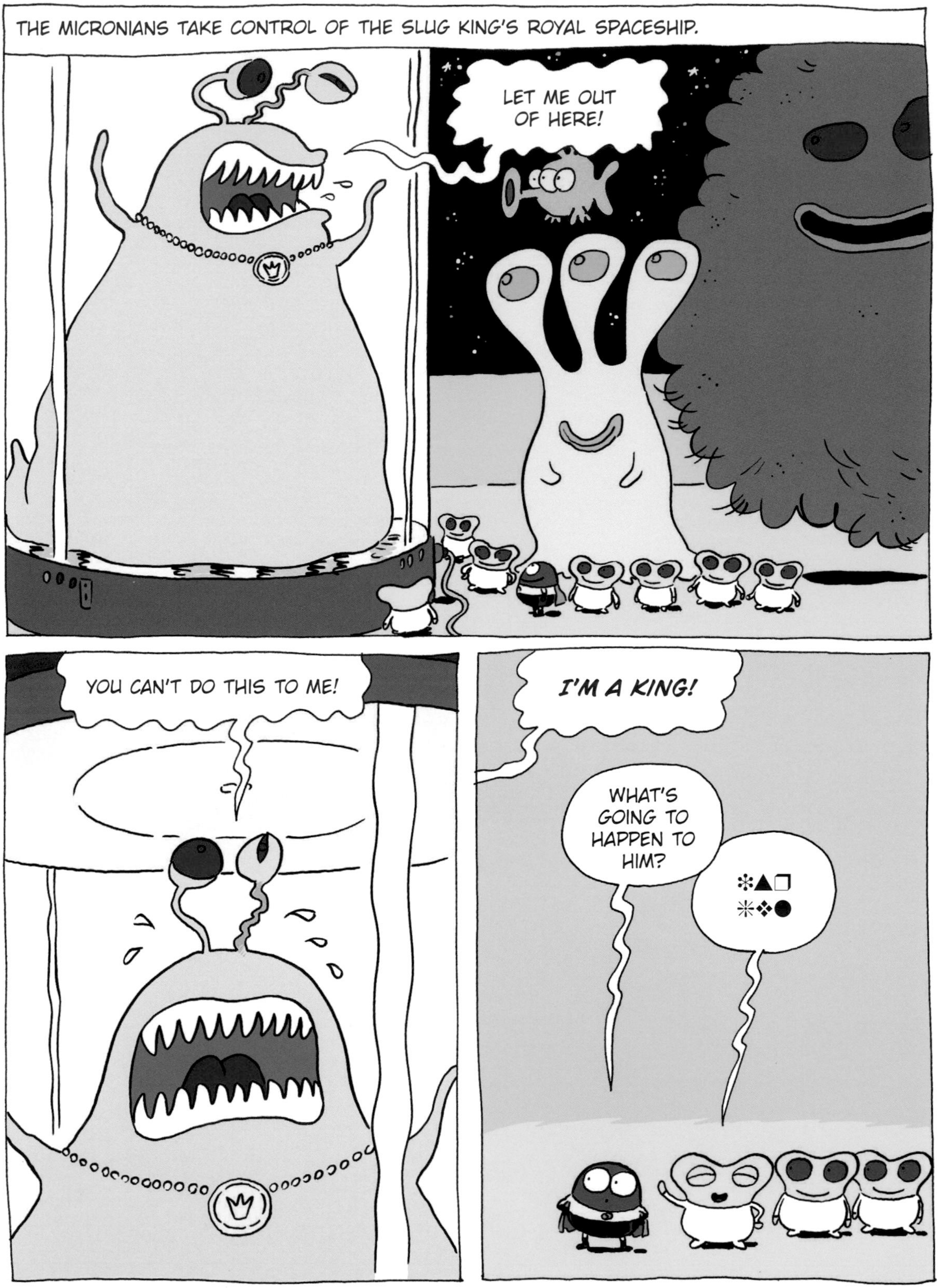
THE MICRONIANS TAKE CONTROL OF THE SLUG KING'S ROYAL SPACESHIP.
LET ME OUT OF HERE!
YOU CAN'T DO THIS TO ME!
I'M A KING!
WHAT'S GOING TO HAPPEN TO HIM?

HUH?
HEH.
HEH HEH.
HA HA HA!

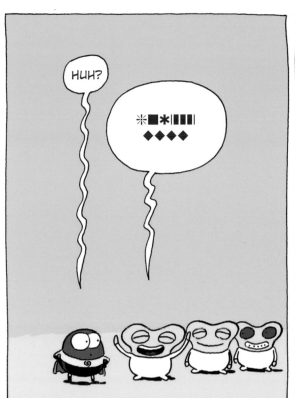

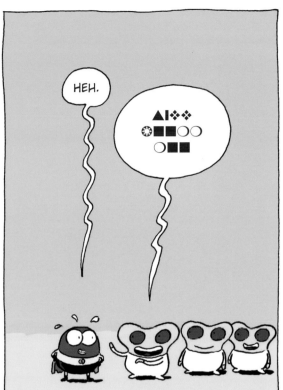

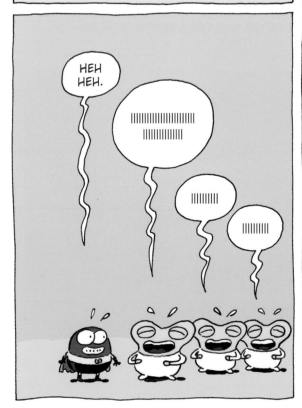

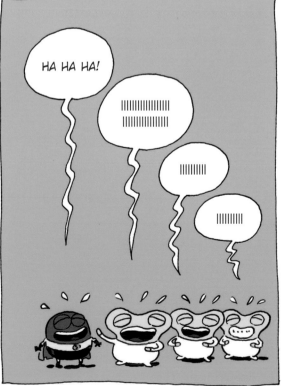

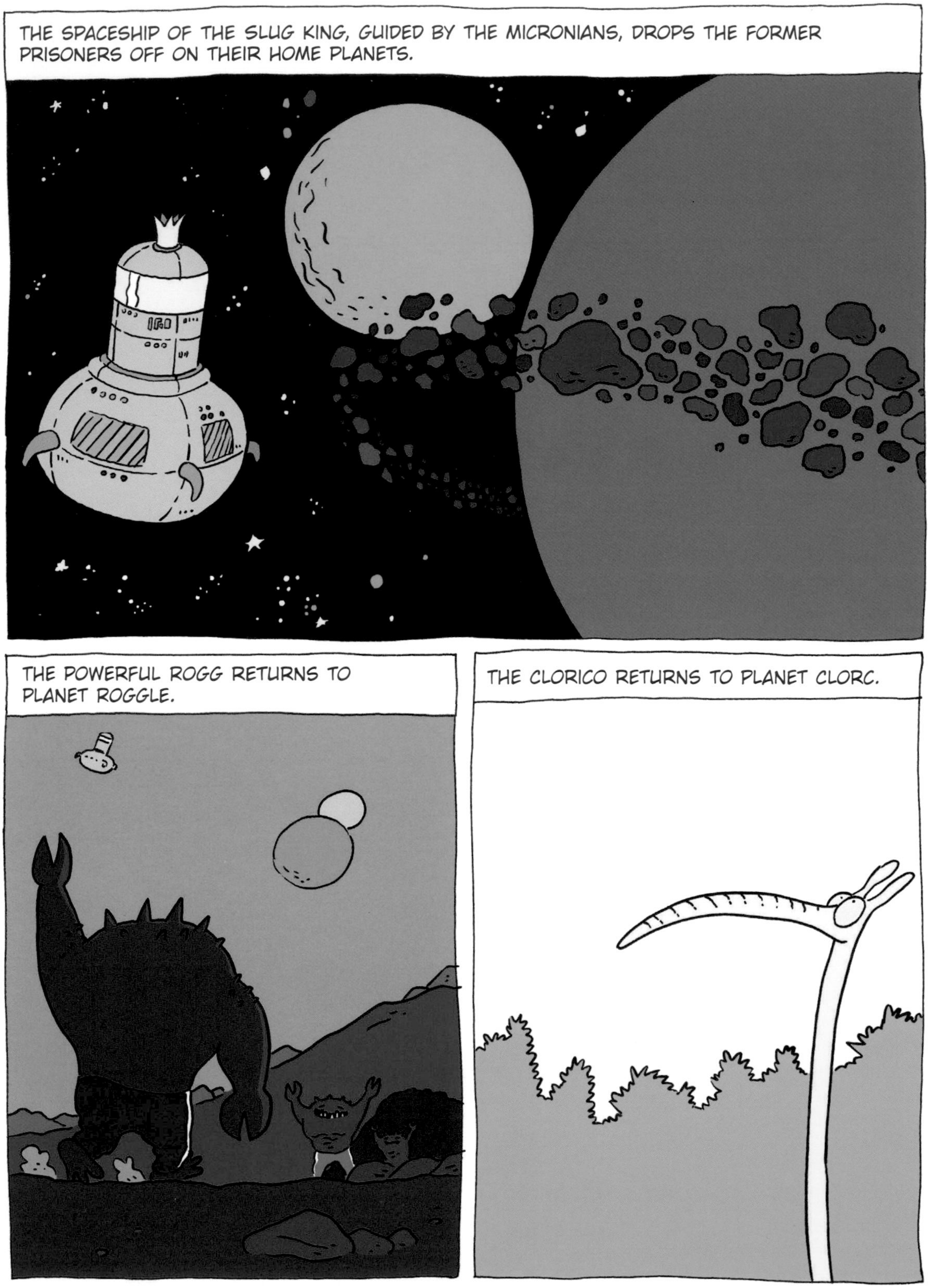
THE SPACESHIP OF THE SLUG KING, GUIDED BY THE MICRONIANS, DROPS THE FORMER PRISONERS OFF ON THEIR HOME PLANETS.
THE POWERFUL ROGG RETURNS TO PLANET ROGGLE.
THE CLORICO RETURNS TO PLANET CLORC.

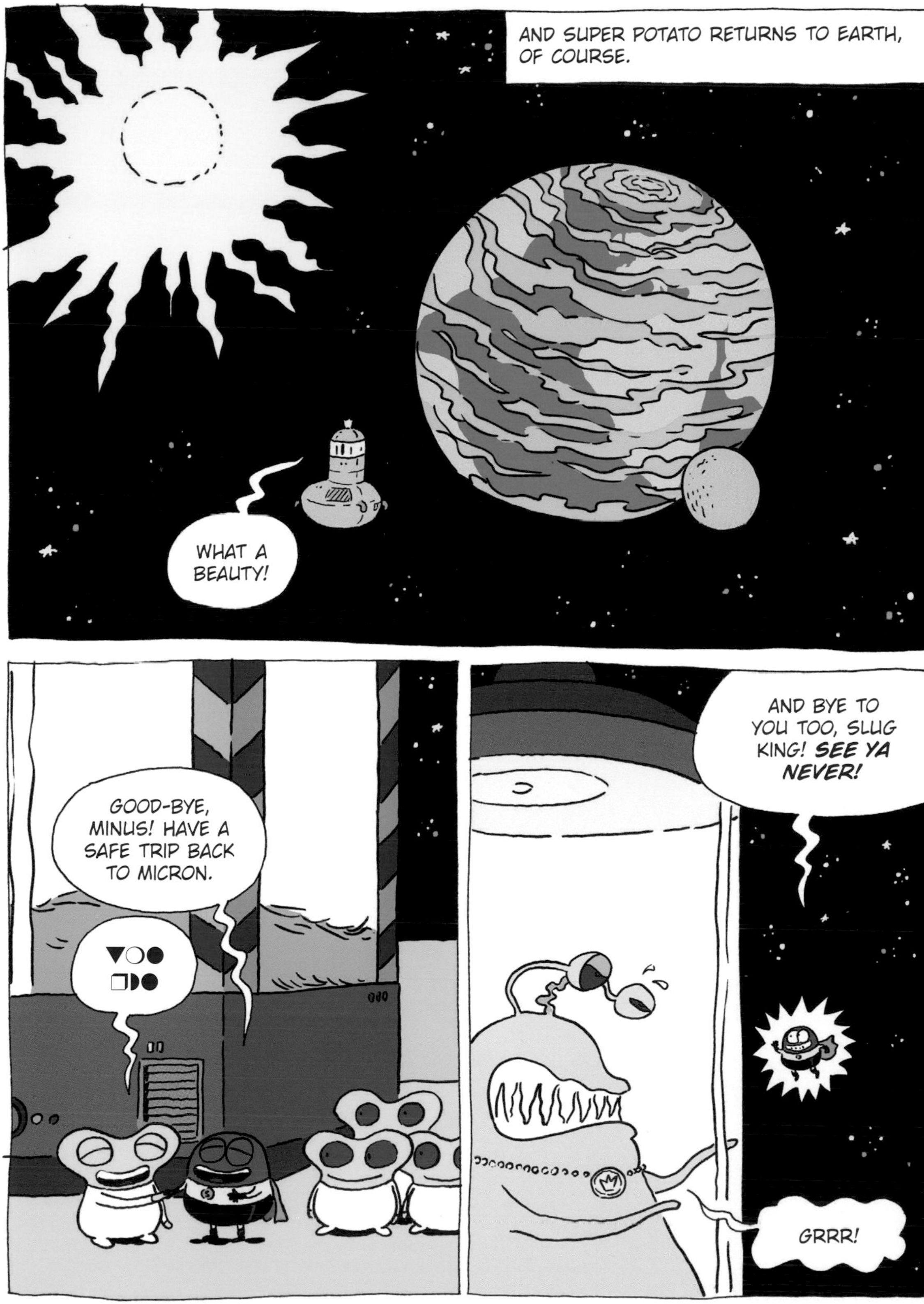
AND SUPER POTATO RETURNS TO EARTH, OF COURSE.
WHAT A BEAUTY!
GOOD-BYE, MINUS! HAVE A SAFE TRIP BACK TO MICRON.
AND BYE TO YOU TOO, SLUG KING! SEE YA NEVER!
GRRR!

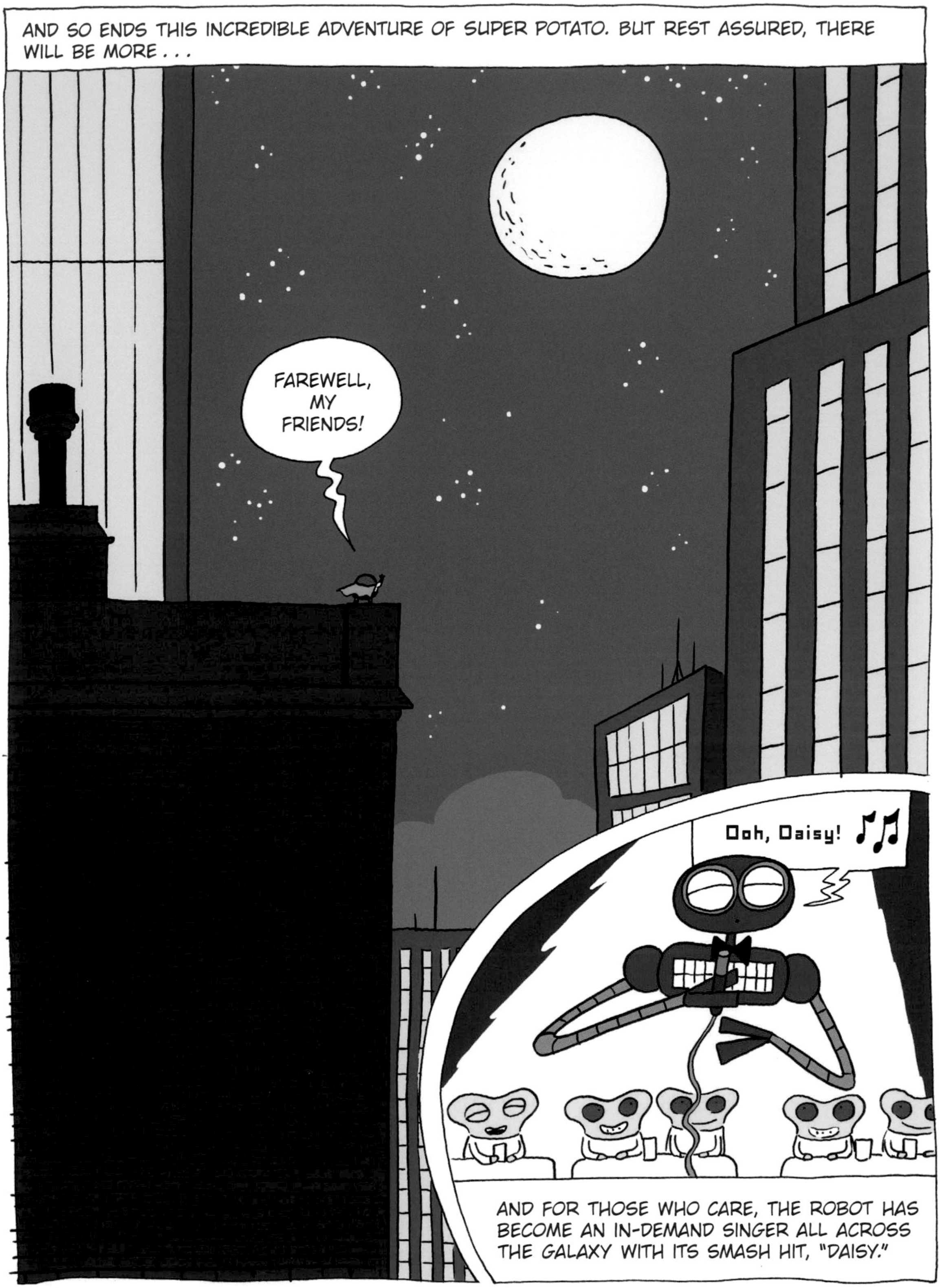
AND SO ENDS THIS INCREDIBLE ADVENTURE OF SUPER POTATO. BUT REST ASSURED, THERE WILL BE MORE . . .
FAREWELL, MY FRIENDS!
Ooh, Daisy!
AND FOR THOSE WHO CARE, THE ROBOT HAS BECOME AN IN-DEMAND SINGER ALL ACROSS THE GALAXY WITH ITS SMASH HIT, "DAISY."

SUPER POTATO

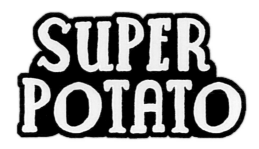

Also available:
The first adventure in the Super Potato saga,

The Epic Origin of Super Potato

SUPER POTATO
#1 THE EPIC ORIGIN OF SUPER POTATO

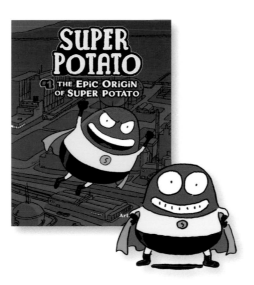

FROM HERO TO POTATO . . . TO HERO AGAIN!

Super Max has it all. He's a superhero with a flashy uniform and a great head of hair. Sure, sometimes the evil Dr. Malevolent pops up to cause trouble. But Super Max has defeated the villain over and over again.

This time is different. This time, Dr. Malevolent's plan works . . . and he turns the handsome hero into a tiny tuber! But there's one thing the doctor didn't count on. The potato still has powers, and justice takes many forms. Super Max may be gone . . . but it's Super Potato's time to fly!

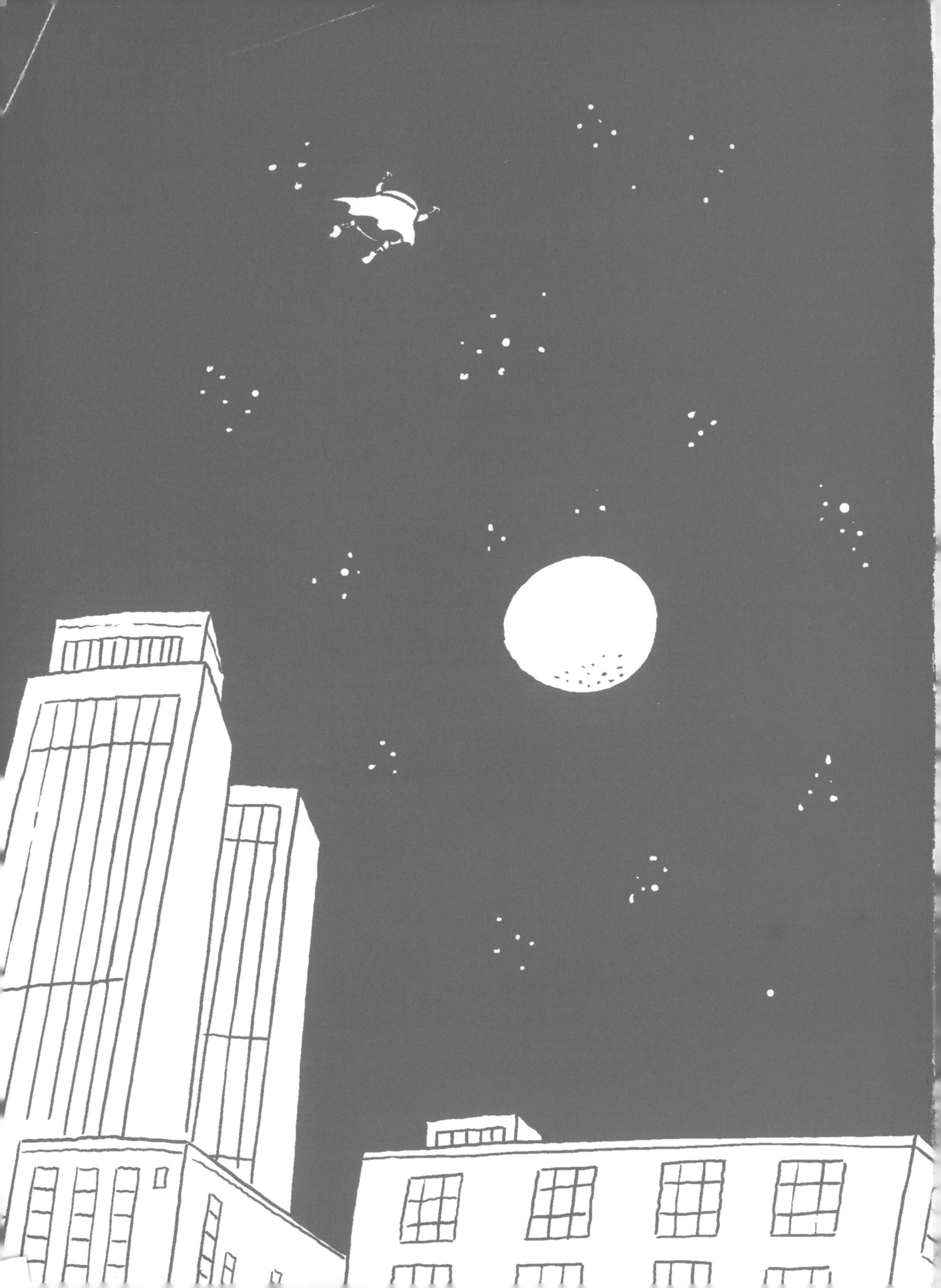